THE SMURFS AND THE MAGIC F

Peyo

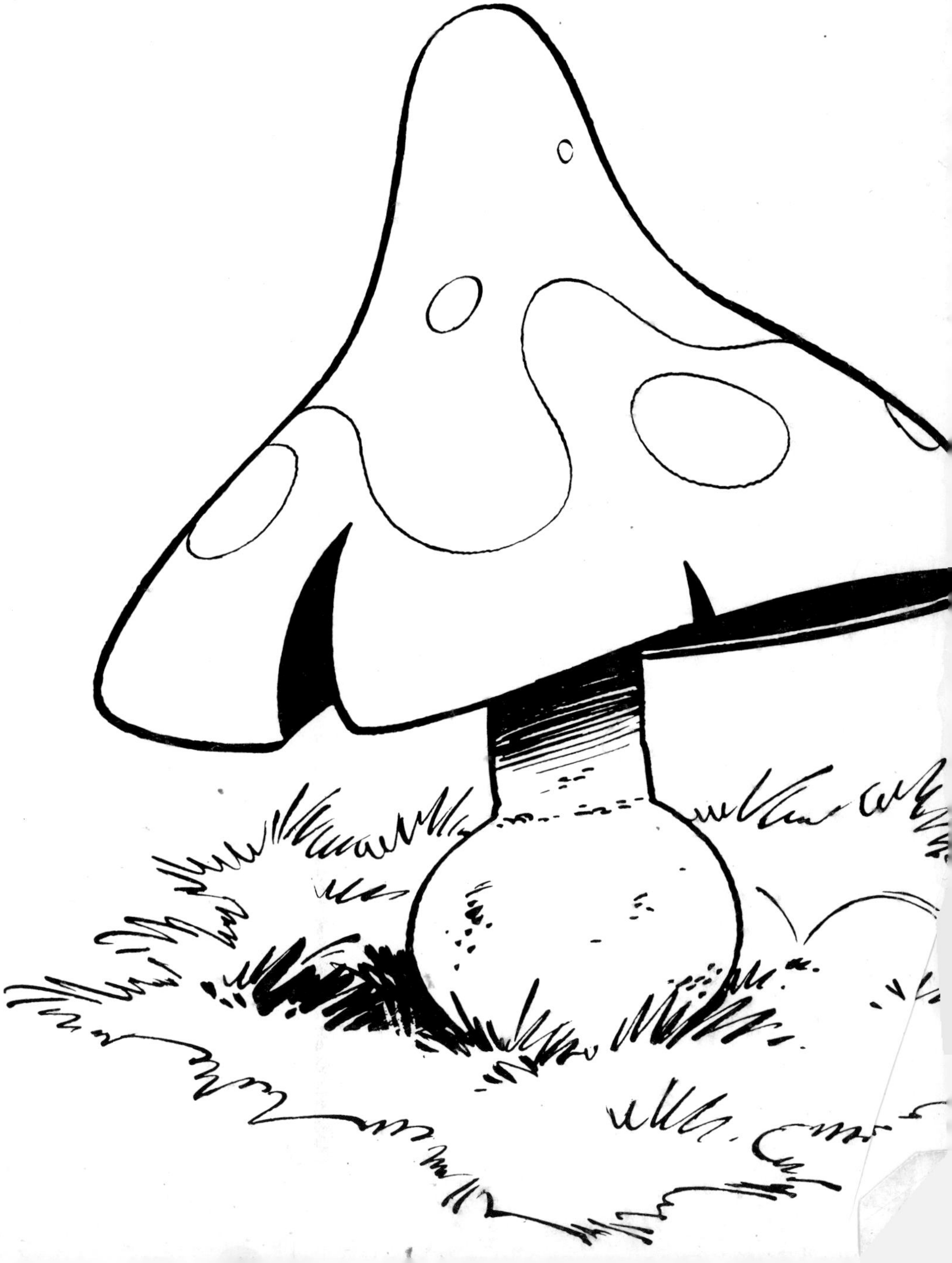

...RFS AND THE MAGIC FLUTE

Look! Two smurfs!
What are they smurfing here?
They sure look smurfy!
Peyo
57

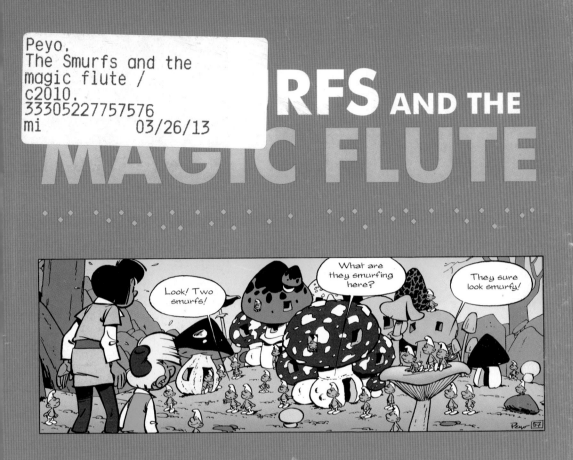

A SMURFS GRAPHIC NOVEL BY Peyo

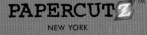

PAPERCUTZ™
NEW YORK

SMURFS GRAPHIC NOVELS AVAILABLE FROM PAPERCUTZ ™

COMING SOON:

The Smurfs graphic novels are available in paperback for $5.99 each and in hardcover for $10.99 each. Available at booksellers everywhere.

Or order from us: please add $4.00 for postage and handling for the first book, add $1.00 for each additional book. Please make check payable to NBM Publishing. Send to: PAPERCUTZ, 40 Exchange Place, Suite 1308 New York, NY 10005
[1-800-886-1223]

WWW.PAPERCUTZ.COM

THE SMURFS AND THE MAGIC FLUTE

SMURF™ © *Peyo* - 2010 - Licensed through Lafig Belgium

English translation Copyright © 2010 by Papercutz.
All rights reserved.

"The Smurfs and the Magic Flute"
 BY YVAN DELPORTE AND PEYO

Joe Johnson, SMURFLATIONS
Adam Grano, SMURFIC DESIGN
Janice Chiang, LETTERING SMURFETTE
Michael Petranek, ASSOCIATE SMURF
Matt. Murray, SMURF CONSULTANT
Jim Salicrup, SMURF-IN-CHIEF

PAPERBACK EDITION ISBN: 978-1-59707-208-3
HARDCOVER EDITION ISBN: 978-1-59707-209-0

PRINTED IN THE USA JULY 2011 BY LIFETOUCH PRINTING
5126 FOREST HILLS CT., LOVES PARK, IL 61111

DISTRIBUTED BY MACMILLAN
THIRD PAPERCUTZ PRINTING

THE SMURFS AND THE MAGIC FLUTE

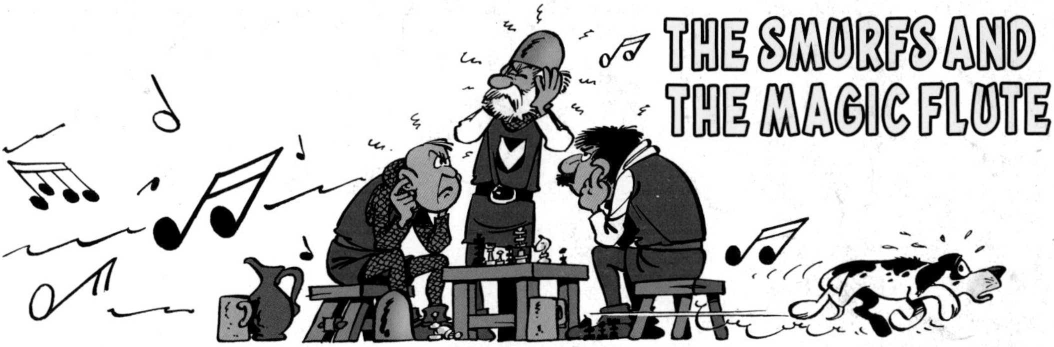

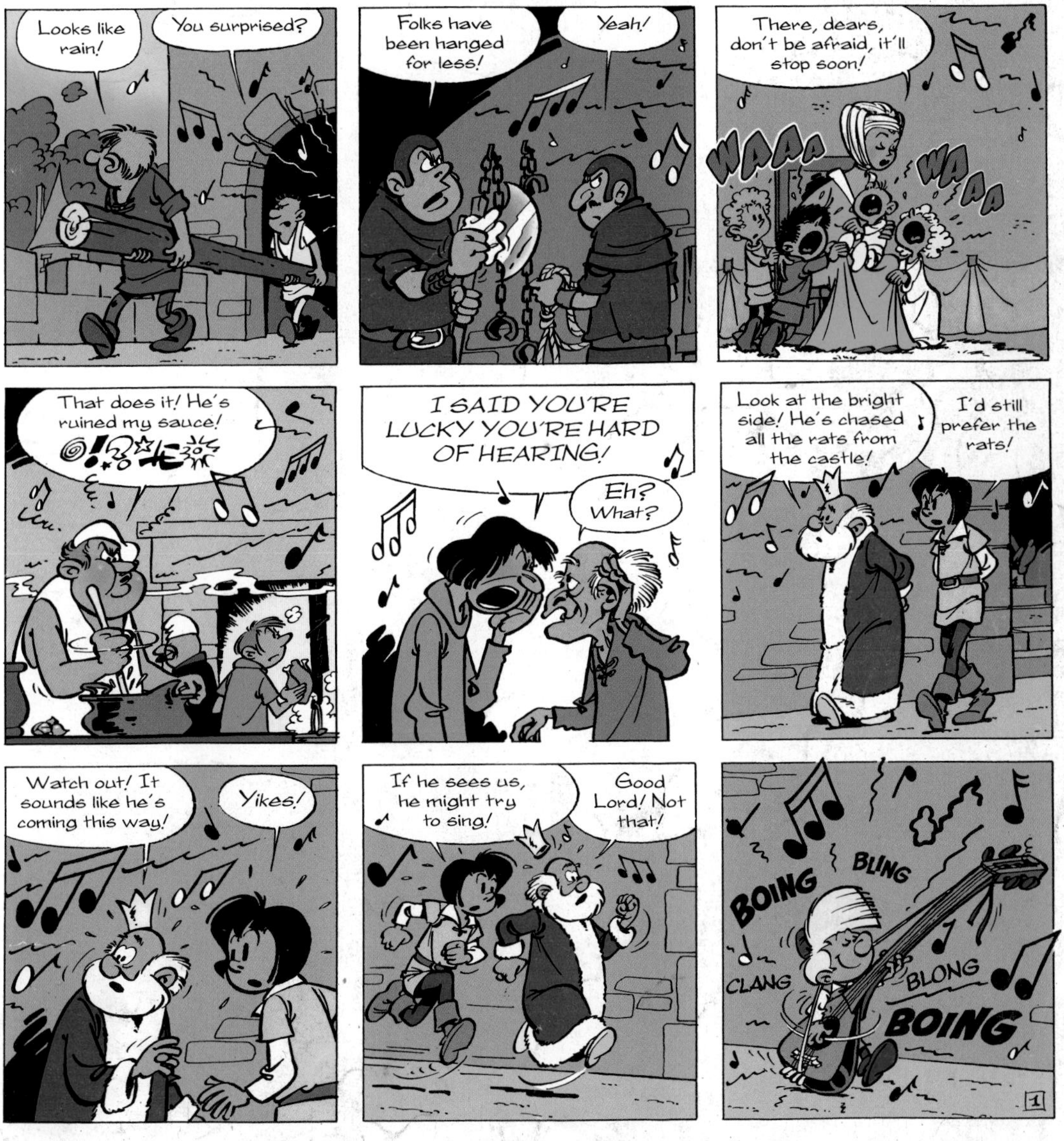

Looks like rain!
You surprised?
Folks have been hanged for less!
Yeah!
There, dears, don't be afraid, it'll stop soon!
WAAA
WAAA
That does it! He's ruined my sauce!
I SAID YOU'RE LUCKY YOU'RE HARD OF HEARING!
Eh? What?
Look at the bright side! He's chased all the rats from the castle!
I'd still prefer the rats!
Watch out! It sounds like he's coming this way!
Yikes!
If he sees us, he might try to sing!
Good Lord! Not that!
BOING
BLING
CLANG
BLONG
BOING
1

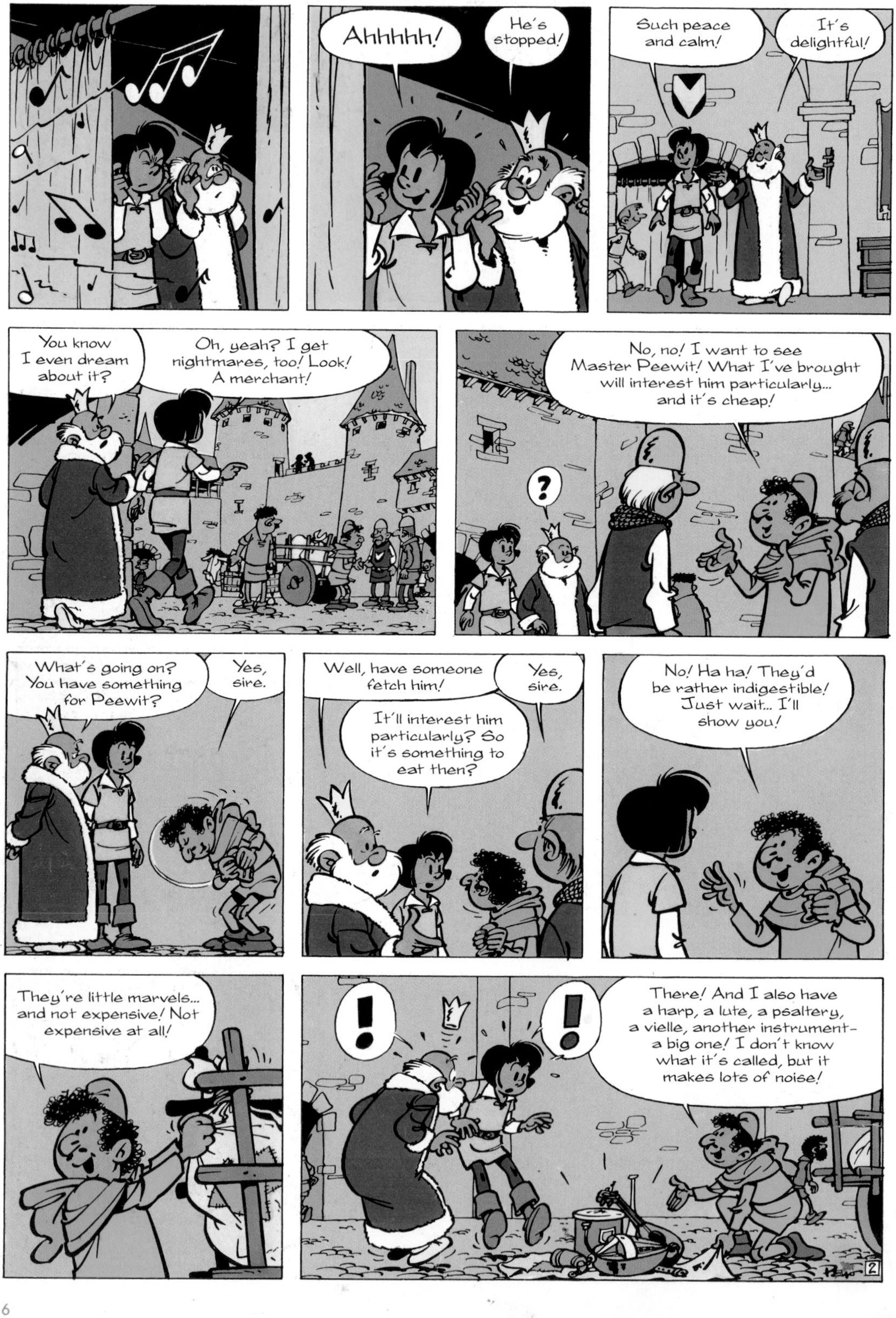

Ahhhhh!
He's stopped!
Such peace and calm!
It's delightful!
You know I even dream about it?
Oh, yeah? I get nightmares, too! Look! A merchant!
No, no! I want to see Master Peewit! What I've brought will interest him particularly... and it's cheap!
?
What's going on? You have something for Peewit?
Yes, sire.
Well, have someone fetch him!
Yes, sire.
It'll interest him particularly? So it's something to eat then?
No! Ha ha! They'd be rather indigestible! Just wait... I'll show you!
They're little marvels... and not expensive! Not expensive at all!
!
!
There! And I also have a harp, a lute, a psaltery, a vielle, another instrument - a big one! I don't know what it's called, but it makes lots of noise!
2

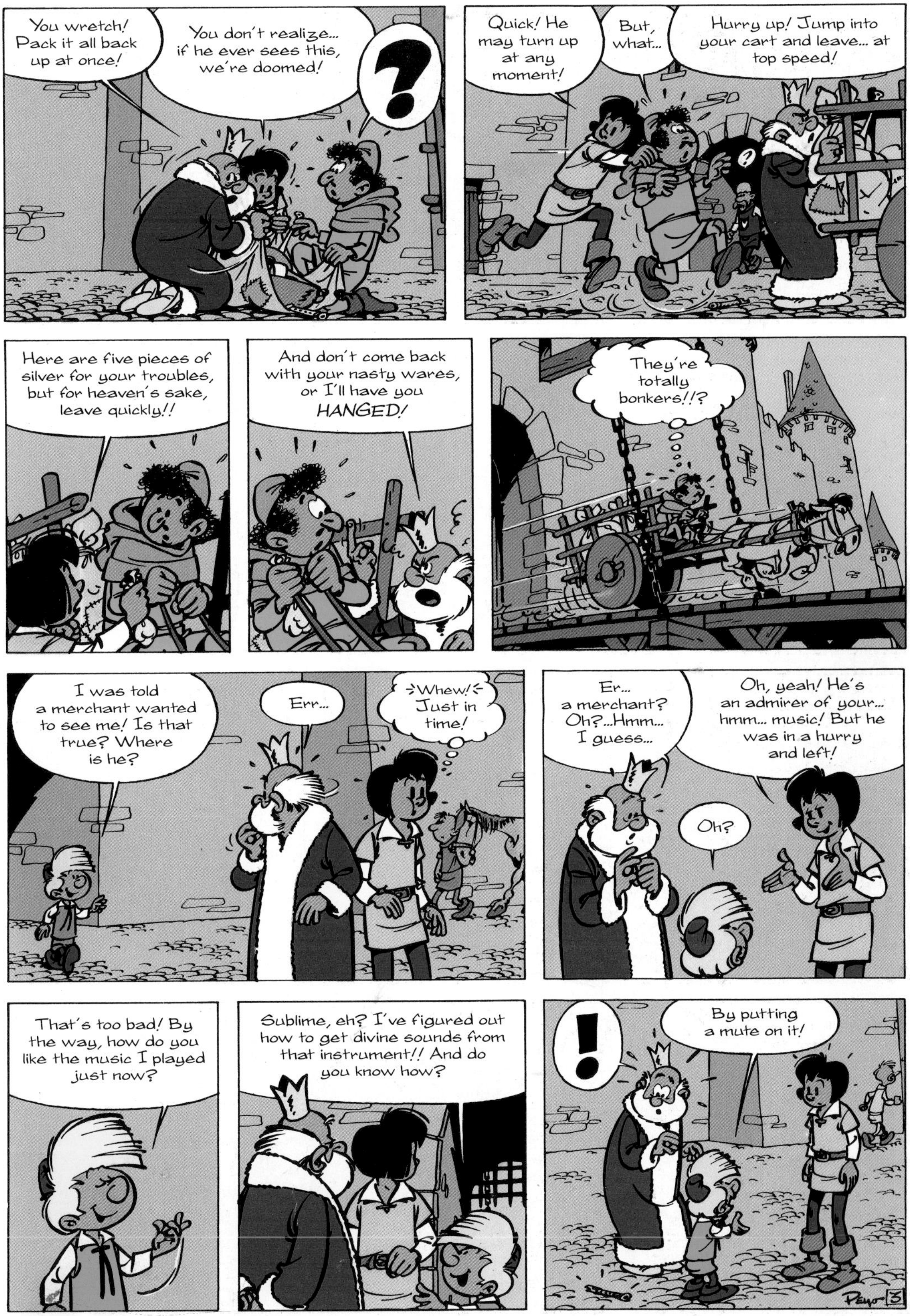
You wretch! Pack it all back up at once!
You don't realize... if he ever sees this, we're doomed!
?
Quick! He may turn up at any moment!
But, what...
Hurry up! Jump into your cart and leave... at top speed!
Here are five pieces of silver for your troubles, but for heaven's sake, leave quickly!!
And don't come back with your nasty wares, or I'll have you HANGED!
They're totally bonkers!!?
I was told a merchant wanted to see me! Is that true? Where is he?
Err...
Whew! Just in time!
Er... a merchant? Oh?...Hmm... I guess...
Oh, yeah! He's an admirer of your... hmm... music! But he was in a hurry and left!
Oh?
That's too bad! By the way, how do you like the music I played just now?
Sublime, eh? I've figured out how to get divine sounds from that instrument!! And do you know how?
!
By putting a mute on it!
Peyo 3

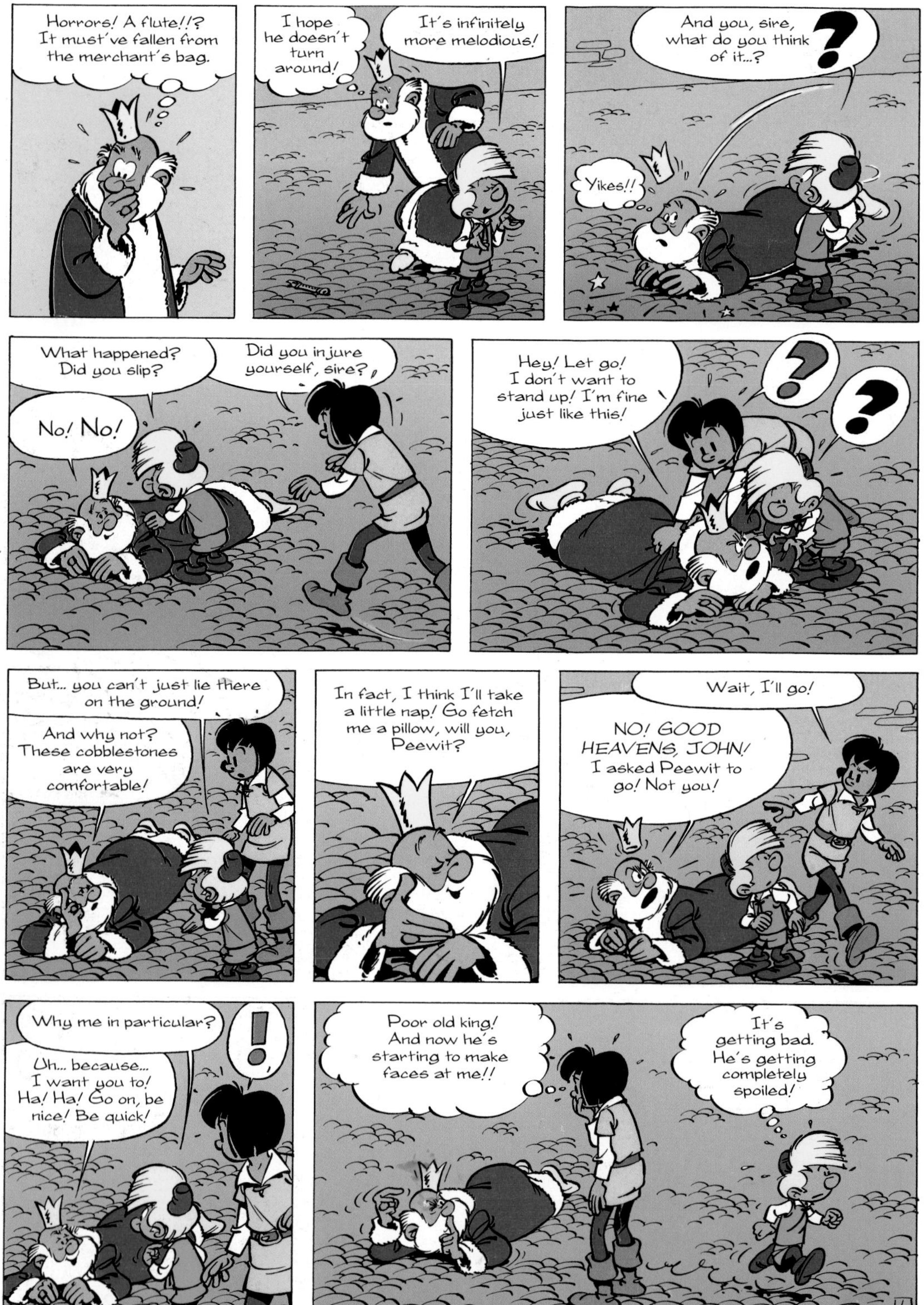
Horrors! A flute!!? It must've fallen from the merchant's bag.
I hope he doesn't turn around!
It's infinitely more melodious!
And you, sire, what do you think of it...?
Yikes!!
What happened? Did you slip?
Did you injure yourself, sire?
No! No!
Hey! Let go! I don't want to stand up! I'm fine just like this!
But... you can't just lie there on the ground!
And why not? These cobblestones are very comfortable!
In fact, I think I'll take a little nap! Go fetch me a pillow, will you, Peewit?
Wait, I'll go!
NO! GOOD HEAVENS, JOHN! I asked Peewit to go! Not you!
Why me in particular?
Uh... because... I want you to! Ha! Ha! Go on, be nice! Be quick!
Poor old king! And now he's starting to make faces at me!!
It's getting bad. He's getting completely spoiled!
Peyo
4

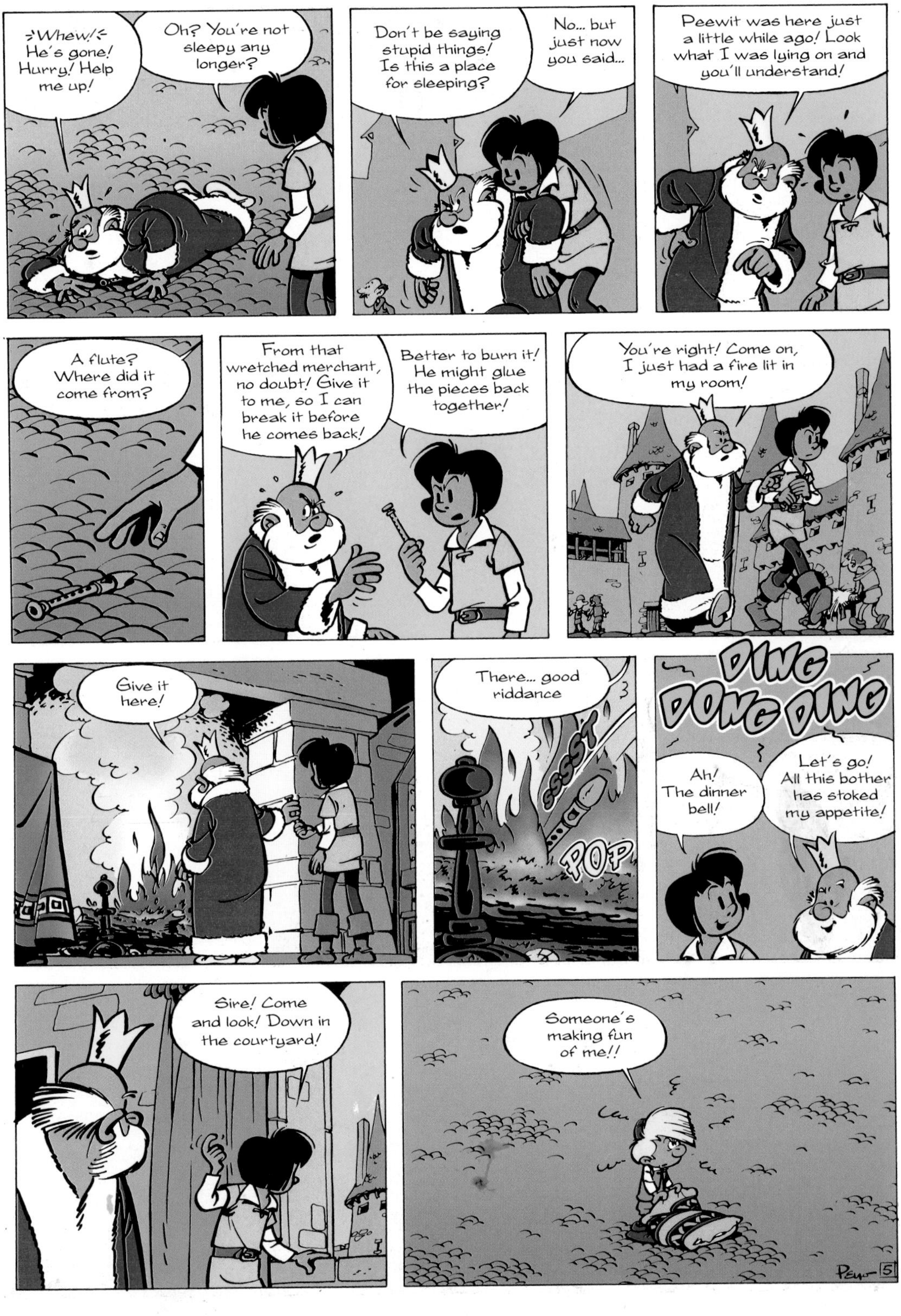
Whew! He's gone! Hurry! Help me up!
Oh? You're not sleepy any longer?
Don't be saying stupid things! Is this a place for sleeping?
No... but just now you said...
Peewit was here just a little while ago! Look what I was lying on and you'll understand!
A flute? Where did it come from?
From that wretched merchant, no doubt! Give it to me, so I can break it before he comes back!
Better to burn it! He might glue the pieces back together!
You're right! Come on, I just had a fire lit in my room!
Give it here!
There... good riddance
SSSST
POP
DING DONG DING
Ah! The dinner bell!
Let's go! All this bother has stoked my appetite!
Sire! Come and look! Down in the courtyard!
Someone's making fun of me!!
5

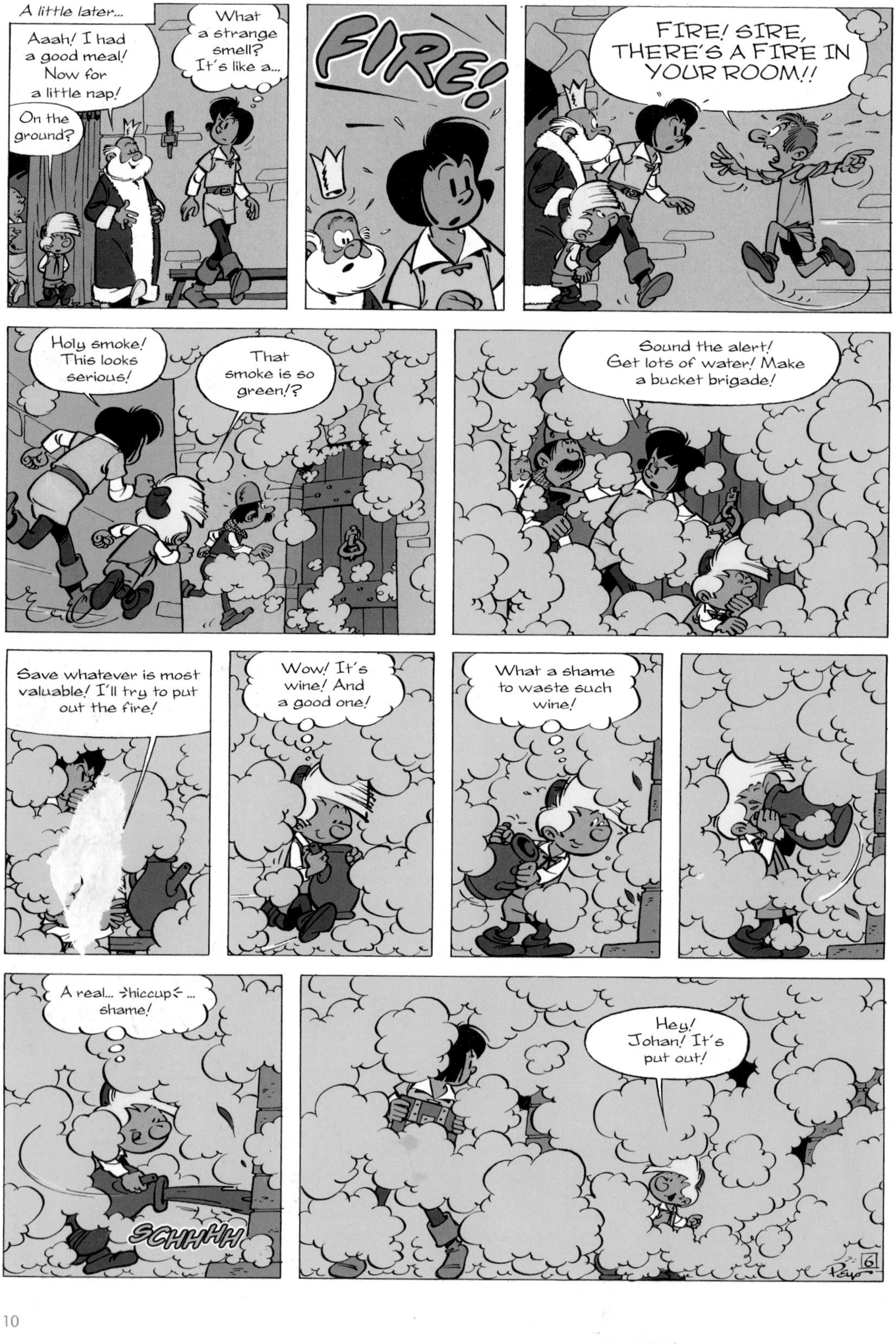
A little later...
Aaah! I had a good meal! Now for a little nap!
On the ground?
What a strange smell? It's like a...
FIRE!
FIRE! SIRE, THERE'S A FIRE IN YOUR ROOM!!
Holy smoke! This looks serious!
That smoke is so green!?
Sound the alert! Get lots of water! Make a bucket brigade!
Save whatever is most valuable! I'll try to put out the fire!
Wow! It's wine! And a good one!
What a shame to waste such wine!
A real... ›hiccup‹ ... shame!
SCHHHH
Hey! Johan! It's put out!
6
Peyo

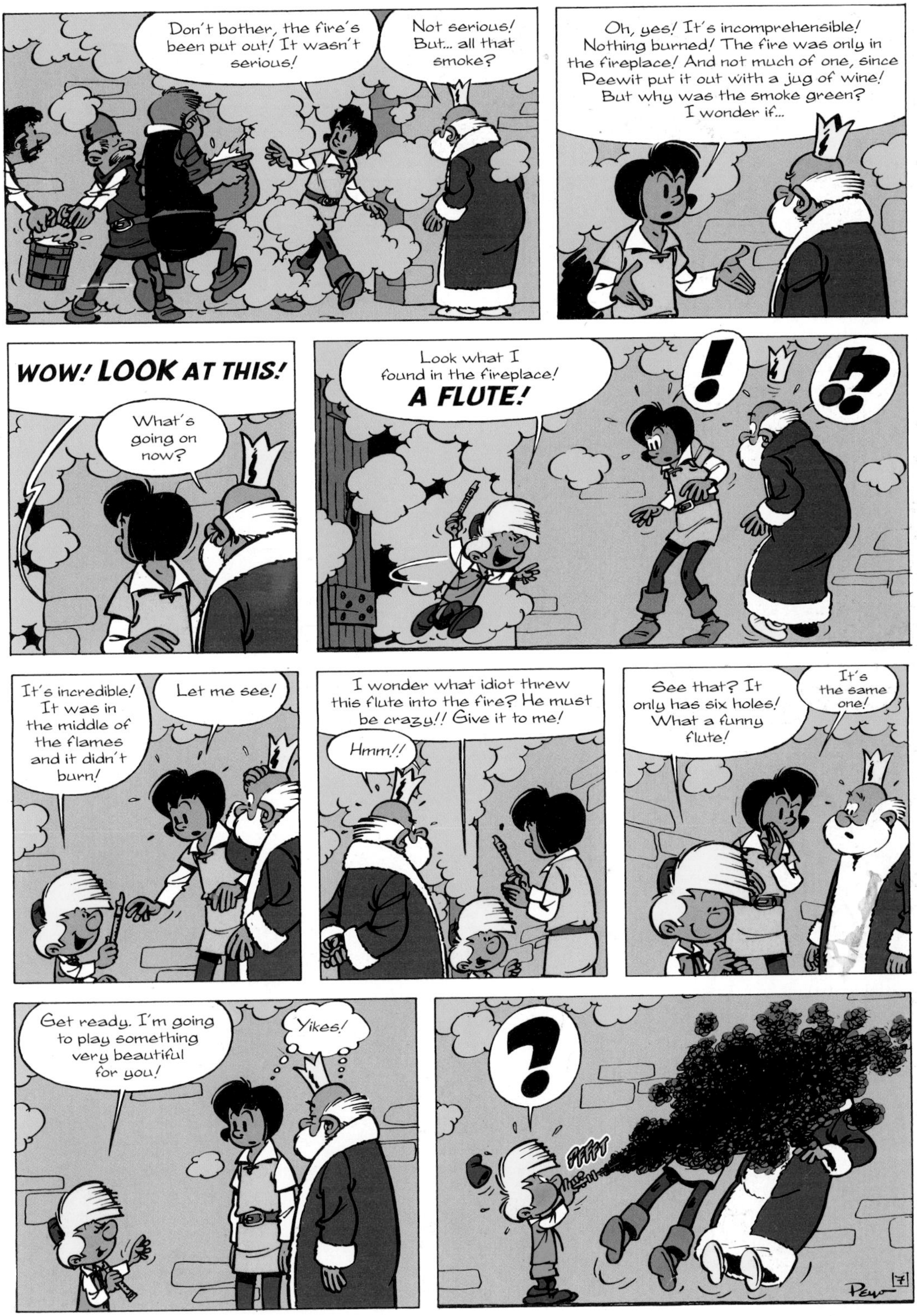
Don't bother, the fire's been put out! It wasn't serious!
Not serious! But... all that smoke?
Oh, yes! It's incomprehensible! Nothing burned! The fire was only in the fireplace! And not much of one, since Peewit put it out with a jug of wine! But why was the smoke green? I wonder if...
WOW! LOOK AT THIS!
What's going on now?
Look what I found in the fireplace! A FLUTE!
It's incredible! It was in the middle of the flames and it didn't burn!
Let me see!
I wonder what idiot threw this flute into the fire? He must be crazy!! Give it to me!
Hmm!!
See that? It only has six holes! What a funny flute!
It's the same one!
Get ready. I'm going to play something very beautiful for you!
Yikes!
PFFT
Peyo
7

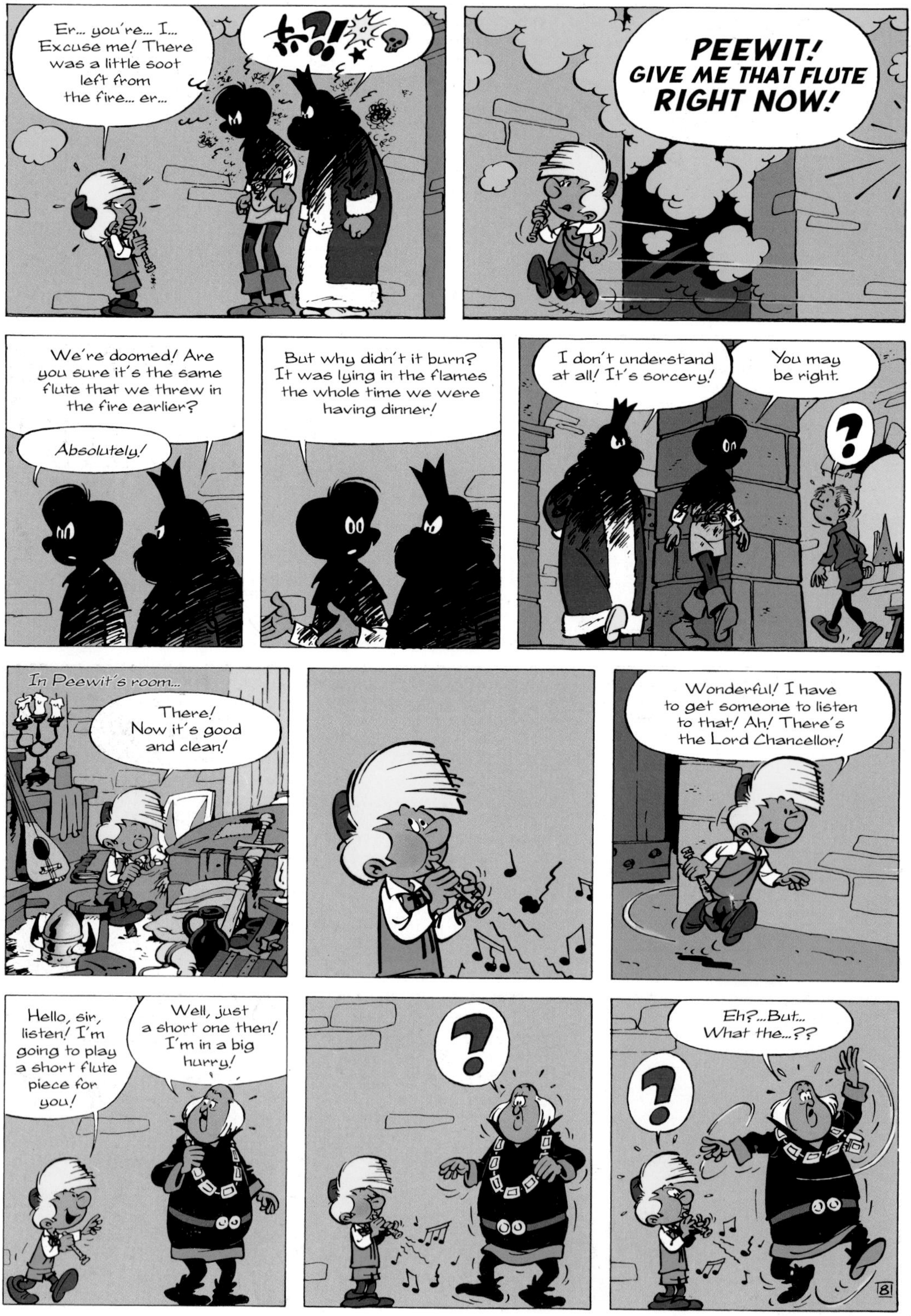
Er... you're... I... Excuse me! There was a little soot left from the fire... er...
PEEWIT! GIVE ME THAT FLUTE RIGHT NOW!
We're doomed! Are you sure it's the same flute that we threw in the fire earlier?
Absolutely!
But why didn't it burn? It was lying in the flames the whole time we were having dinner!
I don't understand at all! It's sorcery!
You may be right.
?
In Peewit's room...
There! Now it's good and clean!
Wonderful! I have to get someone to listen to that! Ah! There's the Lord Chancellor!
Hello, sir, listen! I'm going to play a short flute piece for you!
Well, just a short one then! I'm in a big hurry!
?
?
Eh?...But... What the...??
8

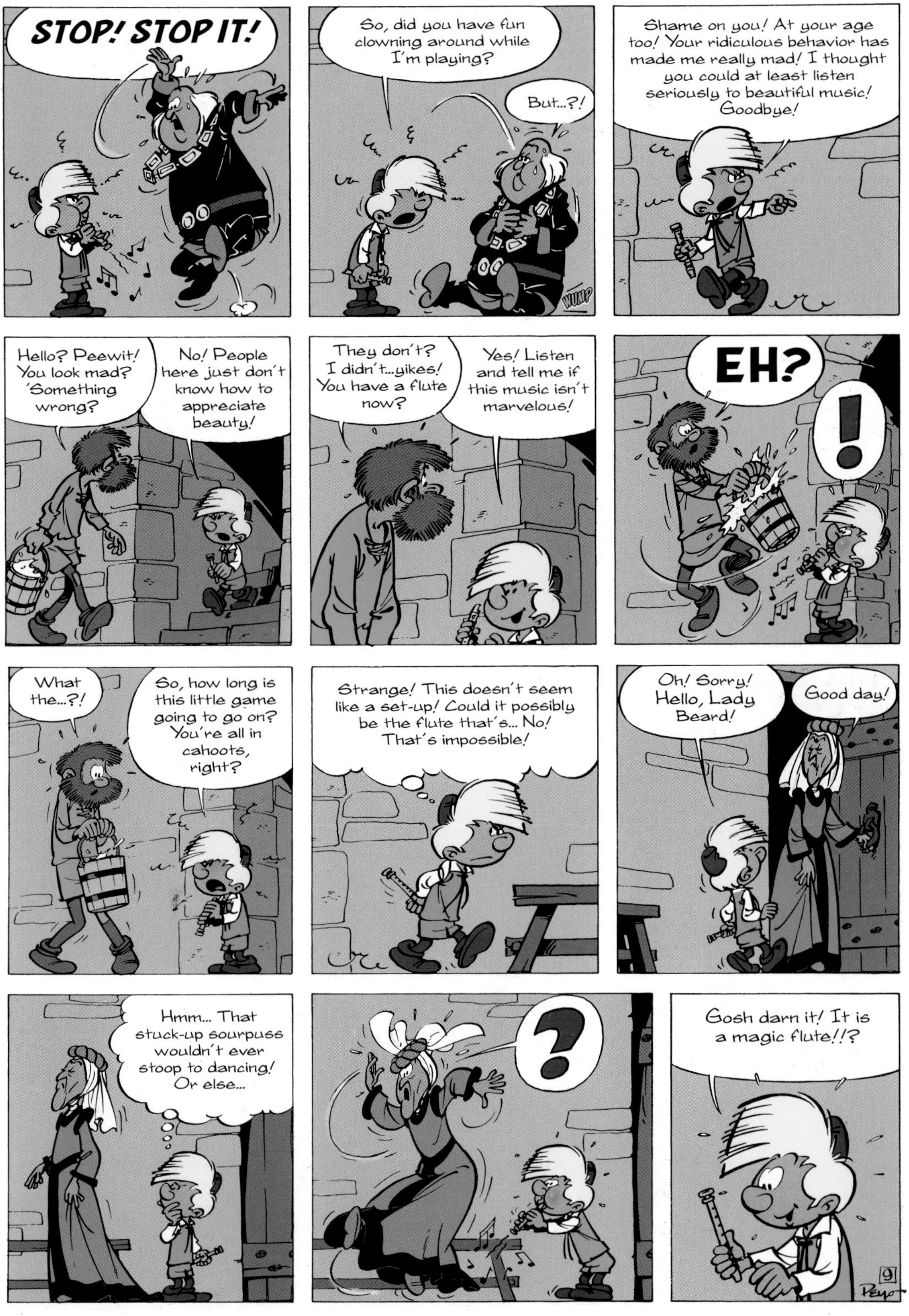
STOP! STOP IT!
So, did you have fun clowning around while I'm playing?
But...?!
WUMP
Shame on you! At your age too! Your ridiculous behavior has made me really mad! I thought you could at least listen seriously to beautiful music! Goodbye!
Hello? Peewit! You look mad? 'Something wrong?
No! People here just don't know how to appreciate beauty!
They don't? I didn't...yikes! You have a flute now?
Yes! Listen and tell me if this music isn't marvelous!
EH?
!
What the...?!
So, how long is this little game going to go on? You're all in cahoots, right?
Strange! This doesn't seem like a set-up! Could it possibly be the flute that's... No! That's impossible!
Oh! Sorry! Hello, Lady Beard!
Good day!
Hmm... That stuck-up sourpuss wouldn't ever stoop to dancing! Or else...
?
Gosh darn it! It is a magic flute!!?
9
Peyo

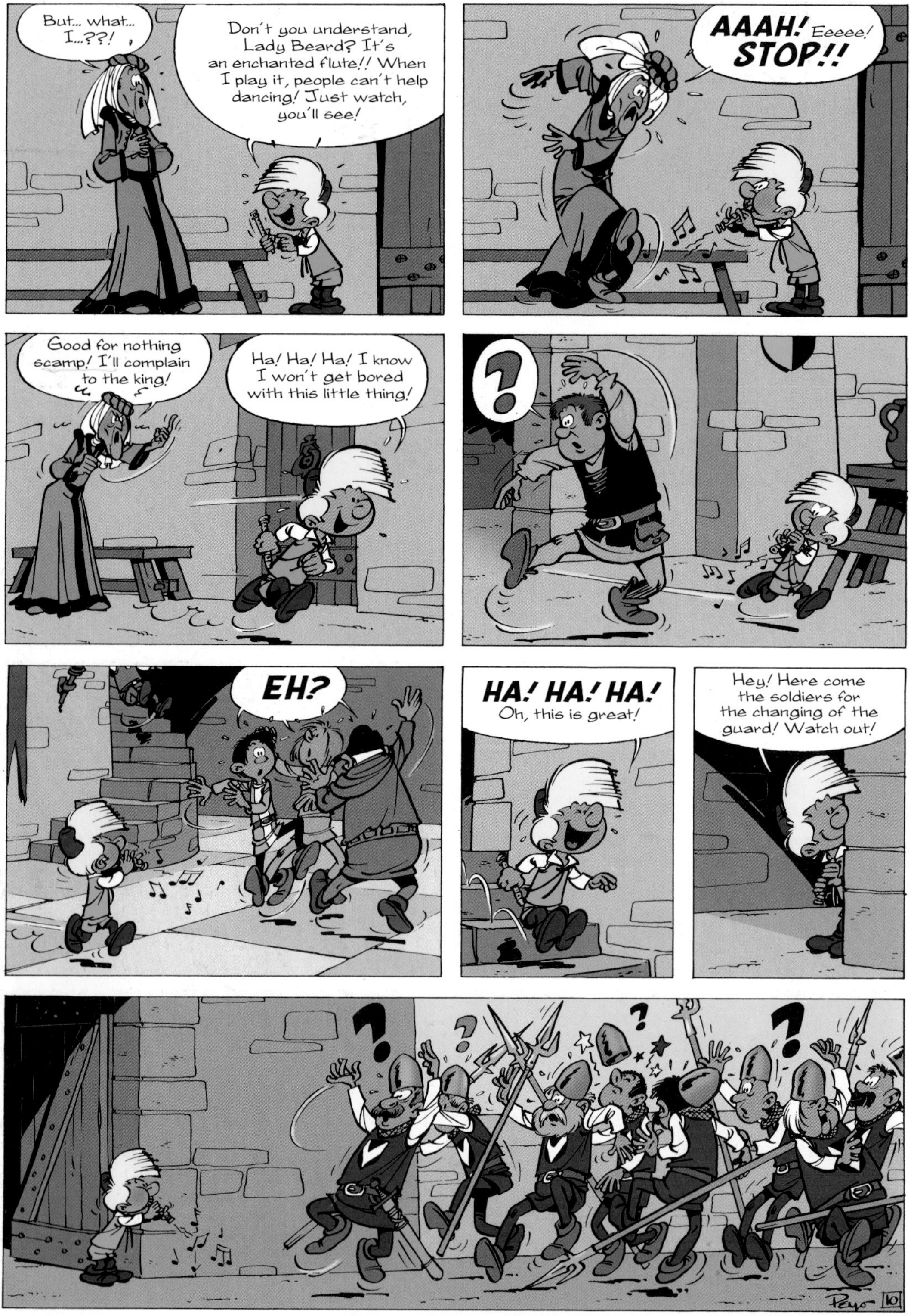
But... what... I...??!
Don't you understand, Lady Beard? It's an enchanted flute!! When I play it, people can't help dancing! Just watch, you'll see!
AAAH! Eeeee! STOP!!
Good for nothing scamp! I'll complain to the king!
Ha! Ha! Ha! I know I won't get bored with this little thing!
?
EH?
HA! HA! HA! Oh, this is great!
Hey! Here come the soldiers for the changing of the guard! Watch out!
?
?
?
?
Peyo
10

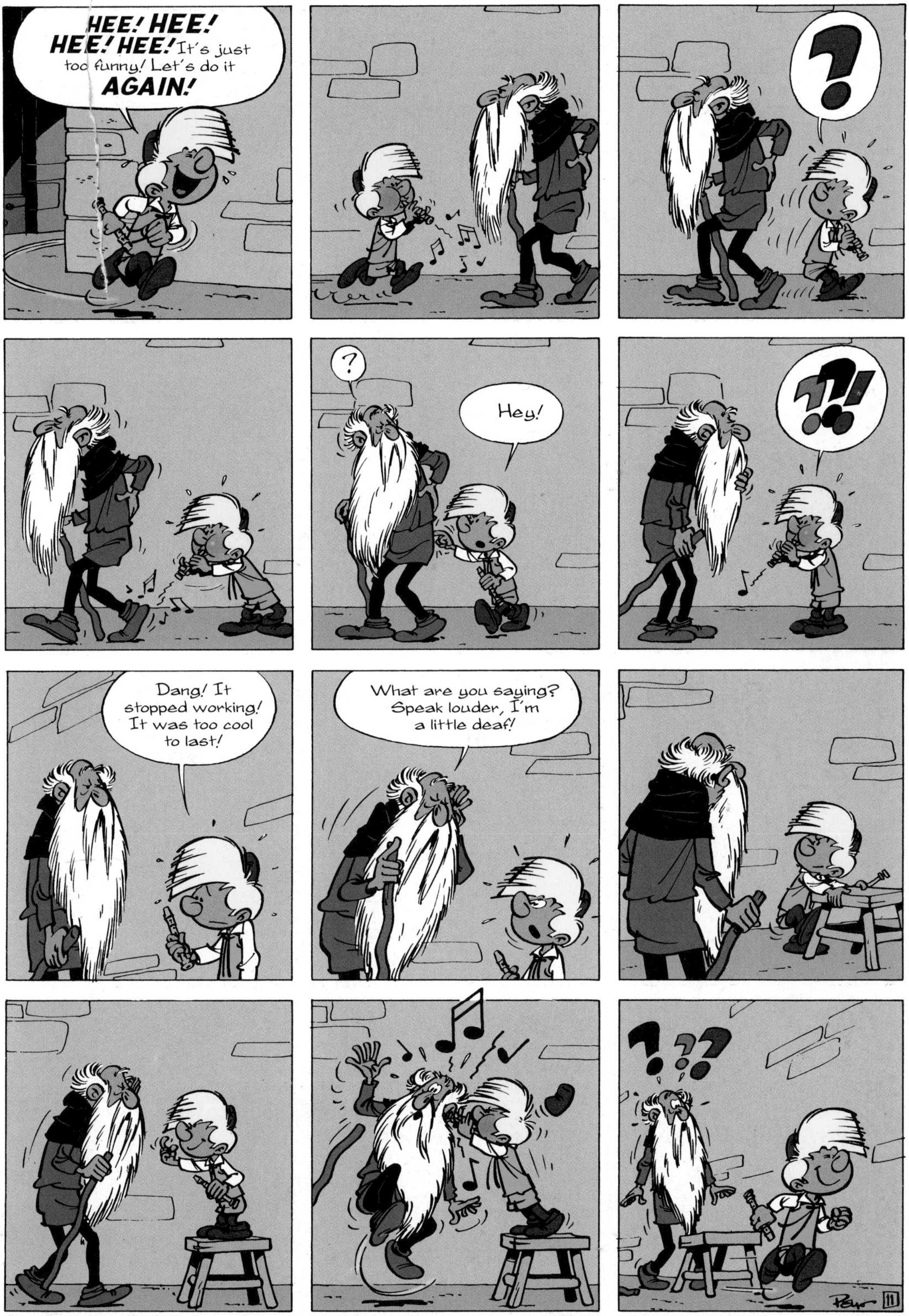
HEE! HEE! HEE! HEE! It's just too funny! Let's do it AGAIN!
?
?
Hey!
?!
Dang! It stopped working! It was too cool to last!
What are you saying? Speak louder, I'm a little deaf!
???

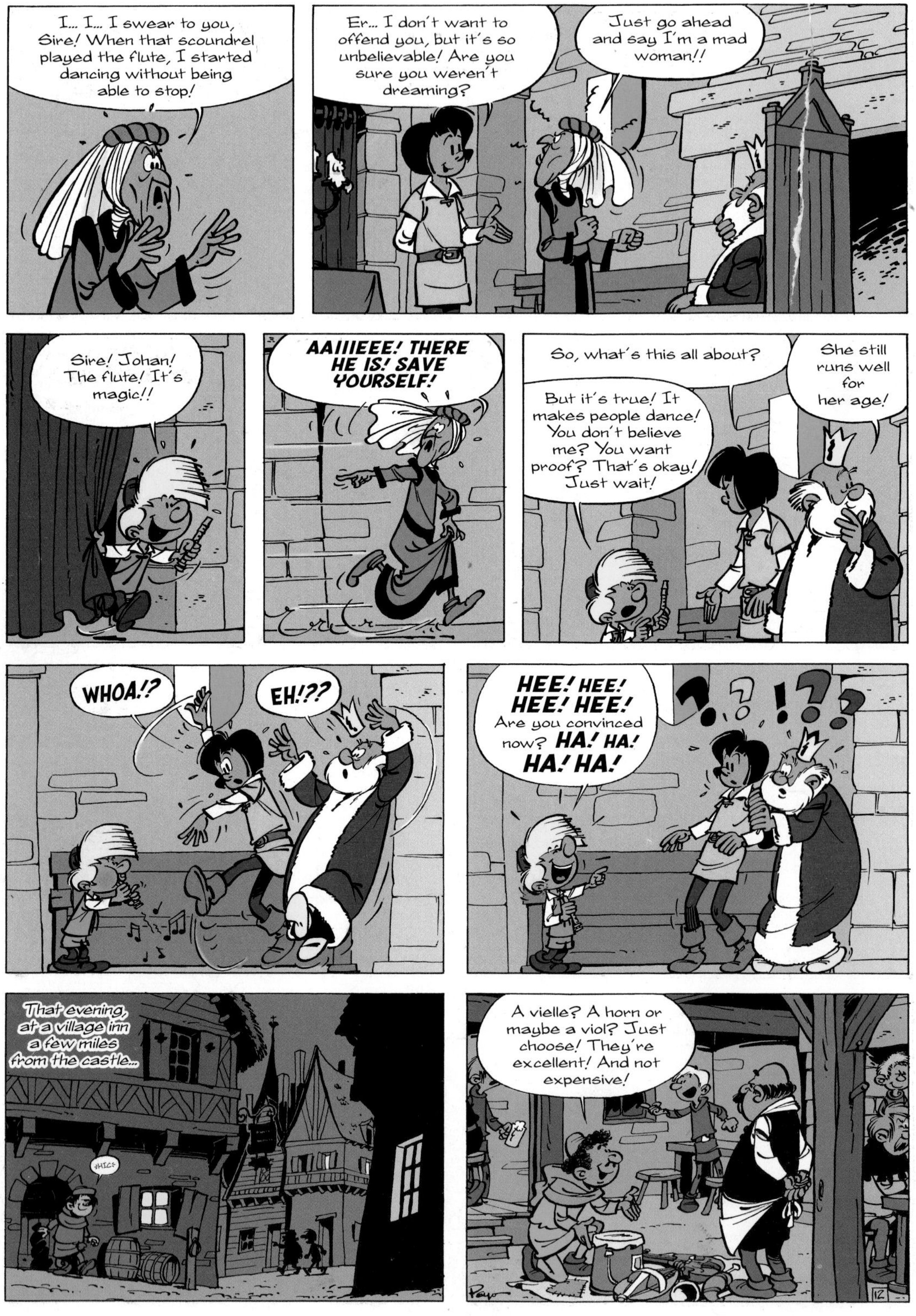

I... I... I swear to you, Sire! When that scoundrel played the flute, I started dancing without being able to stop!
Er... I don't want to offend you, but it's so unbelievable! Are you sure you weren't dreaming?
Just go ahead and say I'm a mad woman!!
Sire! Johan! The flute! It's magic!!
AAIIIEEE! THERE HE IS! SAVE YOURSELF!
So, what's this all about?
She still runs well for her age!
But it's true! It makes people dance! You don't believe me? You want proof? That's okay! Just wait!
WHOA!?
EH!??
HEE! HEE! HEE! HEE! Are you convinced now? HA! HA! HA! HA!
That evening, at a village inn a few miles from the castle...
HIC!
A vielle? A horn or maybe a viol? Just choose! They're excellent! And not expensive!

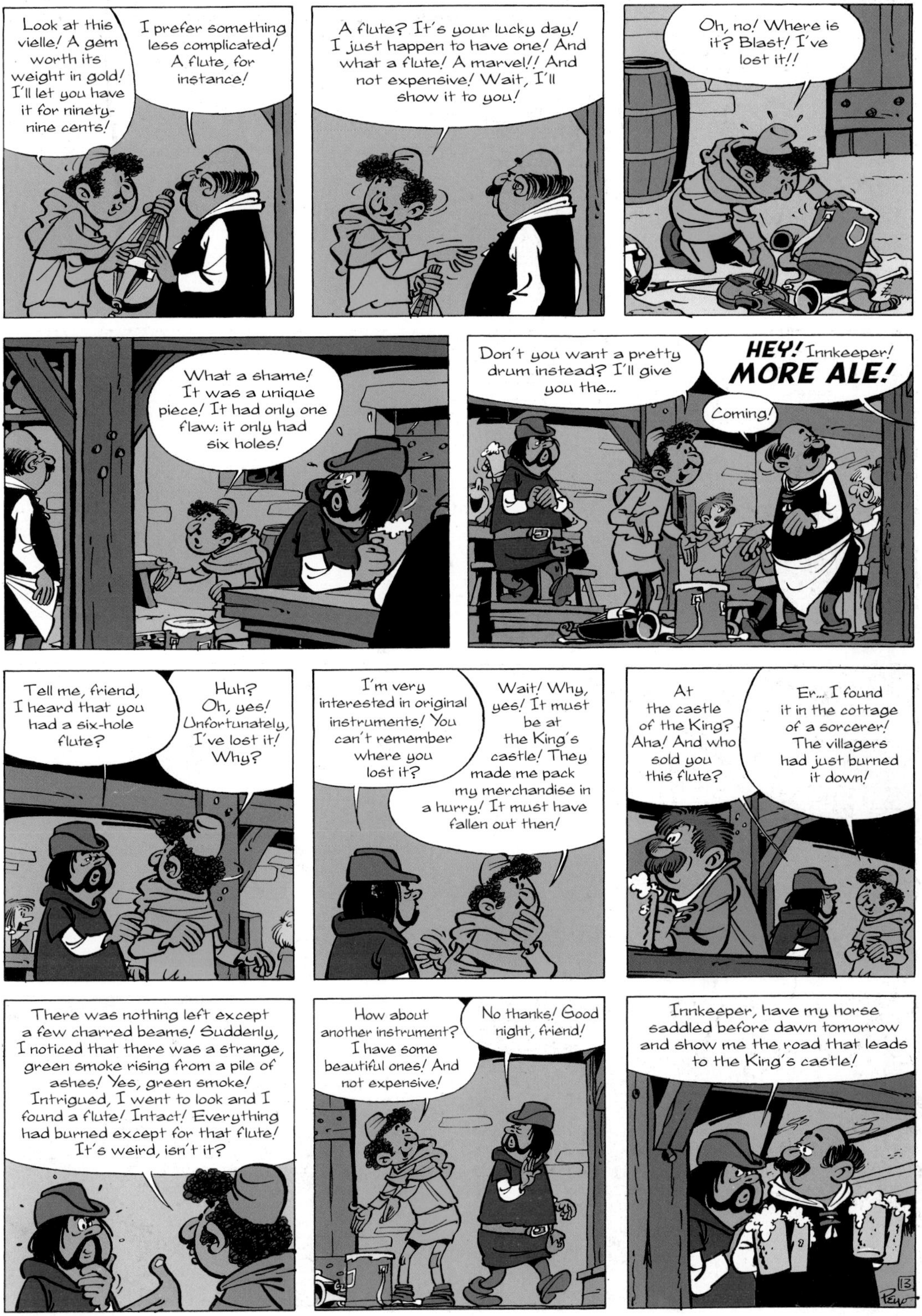

Look at this vielle! A gem worth its weight in gold! I'll let you have it for ninety-nine cents!
I prefer something less complicated! A flute, for instance!
A flute? It's your lucky day! I just happen to have one! And what a flute! A marvel!! And not expensive! Wait, I'll show it to you!
Oh, no! Where is it? Blast! I've lost it!!
What a shame! It was a unique piece! It had only one flaw: it only had six holes!
Don't you want a pretty drum instead? I'll give you the...
HEY! Innkeeper! MORE ALE!
Coming!
Tell me, friend, I heard that you had a six-hole flute?
Huh? Oh, yes! Unfortunately, I've lost it! Why?
I'm very interested in original instruments! You can't remember where you lost it?
Wait! Why, yes! It must be at the King's castle! They made me pack my merchandise in a hurry! It must have fallen out then!
At the castle of the King? Aha! And who sold you this flute?
Er... I found it in the cottage of a sorcerer! The villagers had just burned it down!
There was nothing left except a few charred beams! Suddenly, I noticed that there was a strange, green smoke rising from a pile of ashes! Yes, green smoke! Intrigued, I went to look and I found a flute! Intact! Everything had burned except for that flute! It's weird, isn't it?
How about another instrument? I have some beautiful ones! And not expensive!
No thanks! Good night, friend!
Innkeeper, have my horse saddled before dawn tomorrow and show me the road that leads to the King's castle!
13

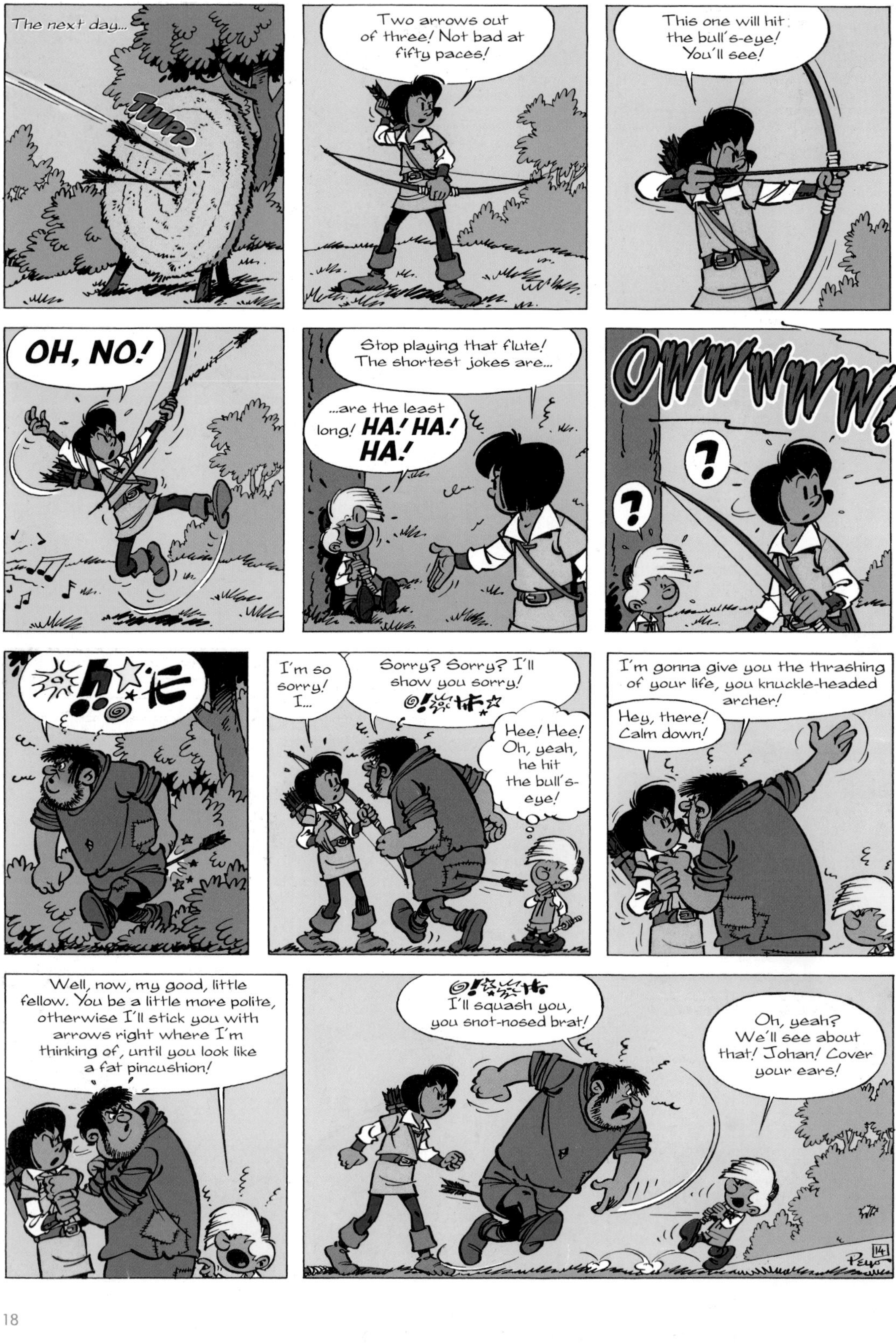
The next day...
THUPP
Two arrows out of three! Not bad at fifty paces!
This one will hit the bull's-eye! You'll see!
OH, NO!
Stop playing that flute! The shortest jokes are...
...are the least long! HA! HA! HA!
OWWWWW!
?
?
I'm so sorry! I...
Sorry? Sorry? I'll show you sorry!
Hee! Hee! Oh, yeah, he hit the bull's-eye!
I'm gonna give you the thrashing of your life, you knuckle-headed archer!
Hey, there! Calm down!
Well, now, my good, little fellow. You be a little more polite, otherwise I'll stick you with arrows right where I'm thinking of, until you look like a fat pincushion!
I'll squash you, you snot-nosed brat!
Oh, yeah? We'll see about that! Johan! Cover your ears!
14
Peyo

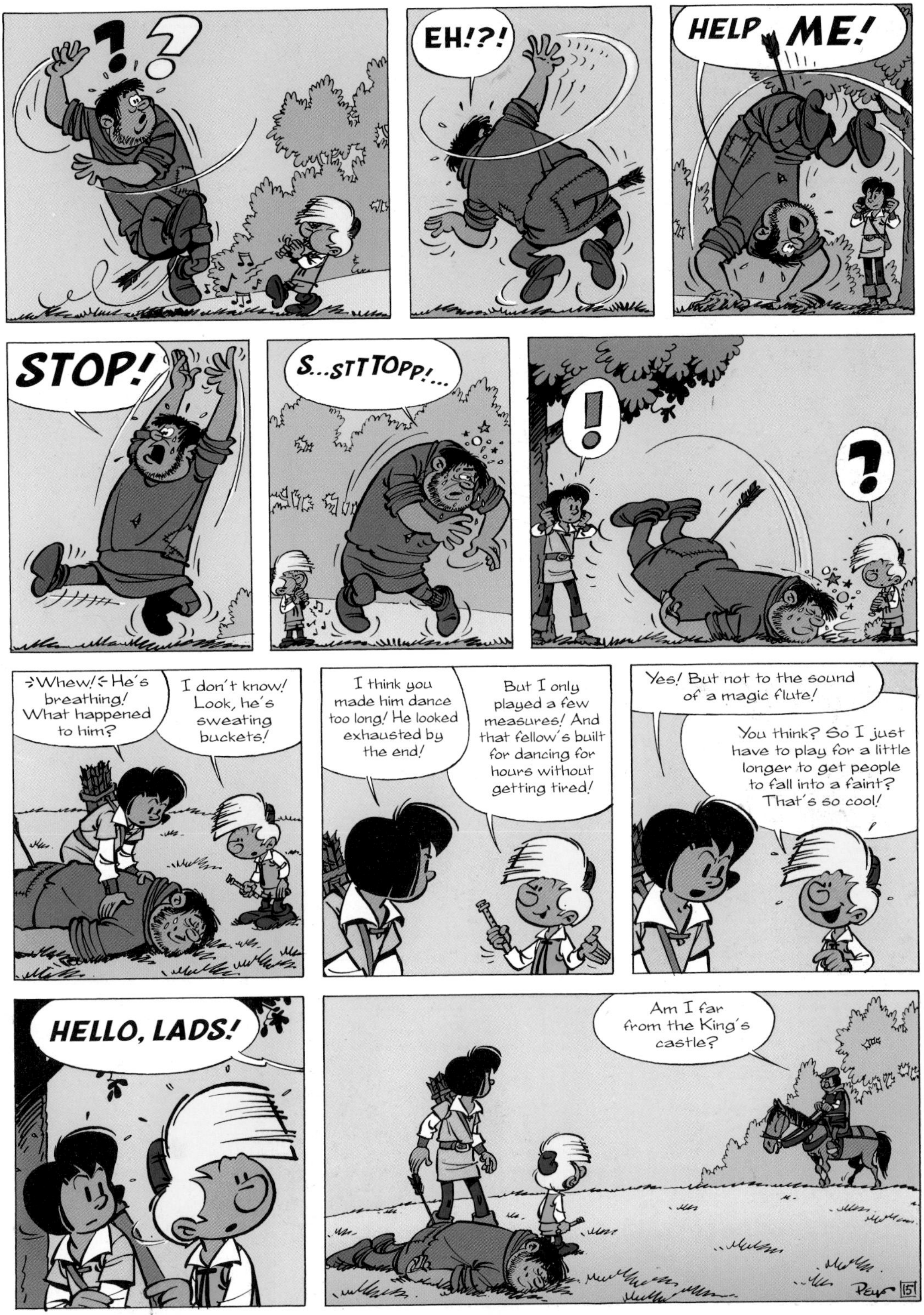
EH!?!
HELP ME!
STOP!
S...STTTOPP!...
!
?
Whew! He's breathing! What happened to him?
I don't know! Look, he's sweating buckets!
I think you made him dance too long! He looked exhausted by the end!
But I only played a few measures! And that fellow's built for dancing for hours without getting tired!
Yes! But not to the sound of a magic flute!
You think? So I just have to play for a little longer to get people to fall into a faint? That's so cool!
HELLO, LADS!
Am I far from the King's castle?
15

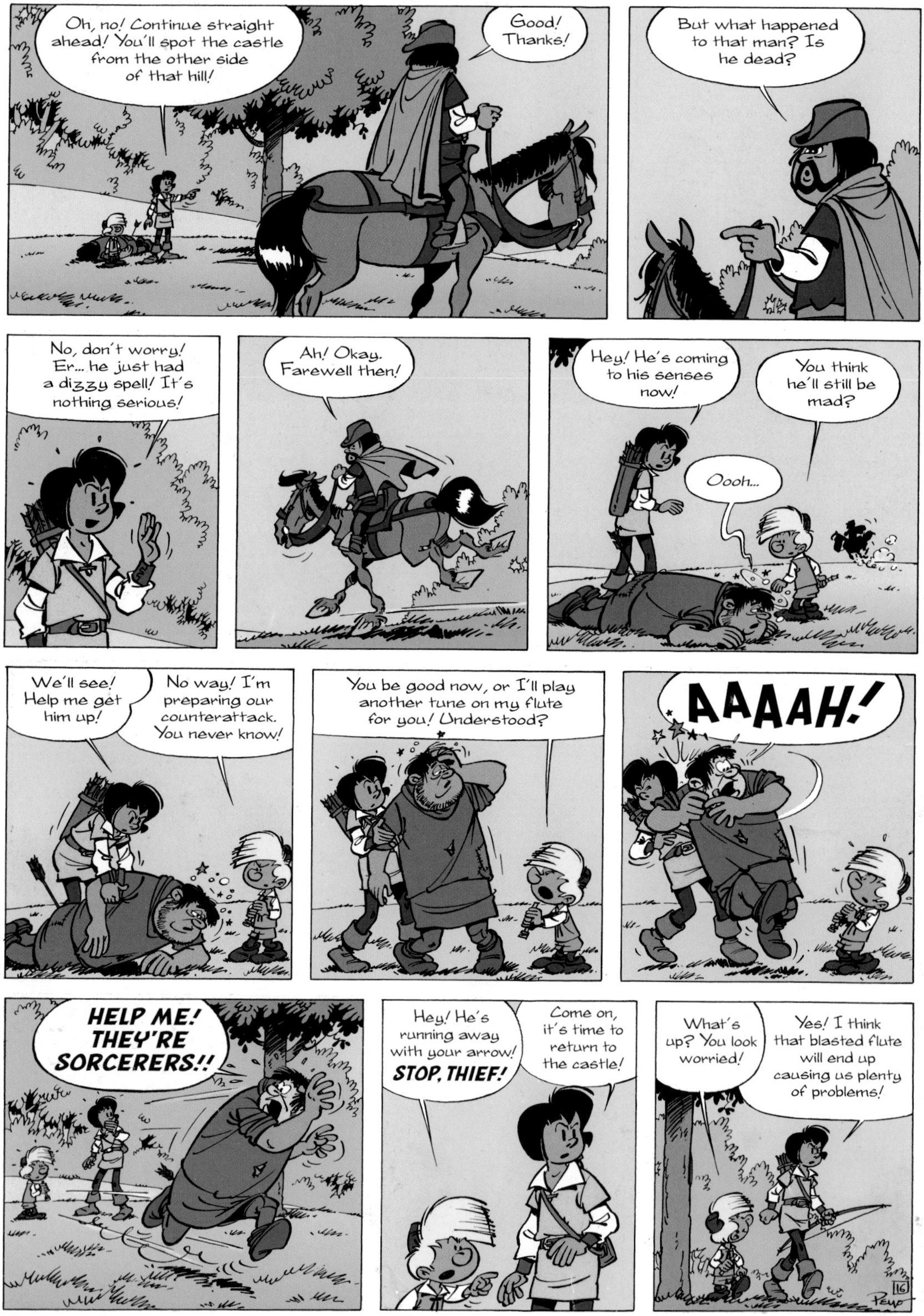
Oh, no! Continue straight ahead! You'll spot the castle from the other side of that hill!
Good! Thanks!
But what happened to that man? Is he dead?
No, don't worry! Er... he just had a dizzy spell! It's nothing serious!
Ah! Okay. Farewell then!
Hey! He's coming to his senses now!
You think he'll still be mad?
Oooh...
We'll see! Help me get him up!
No way! I'm preparing our counterattack. You never know!
You be good now, or I'll play another tune on my flute for you! Understood?
AAAAH!
HELP ME! THEY'RE SORCERERS!!
Hey! He's running away with your arrow! STOP, THIEF!
Come on, it's time to return to the castle!
What's up? You look worried!
Yes! I think that blasted flute will end up causing us plenty of problems!
16
PEYO

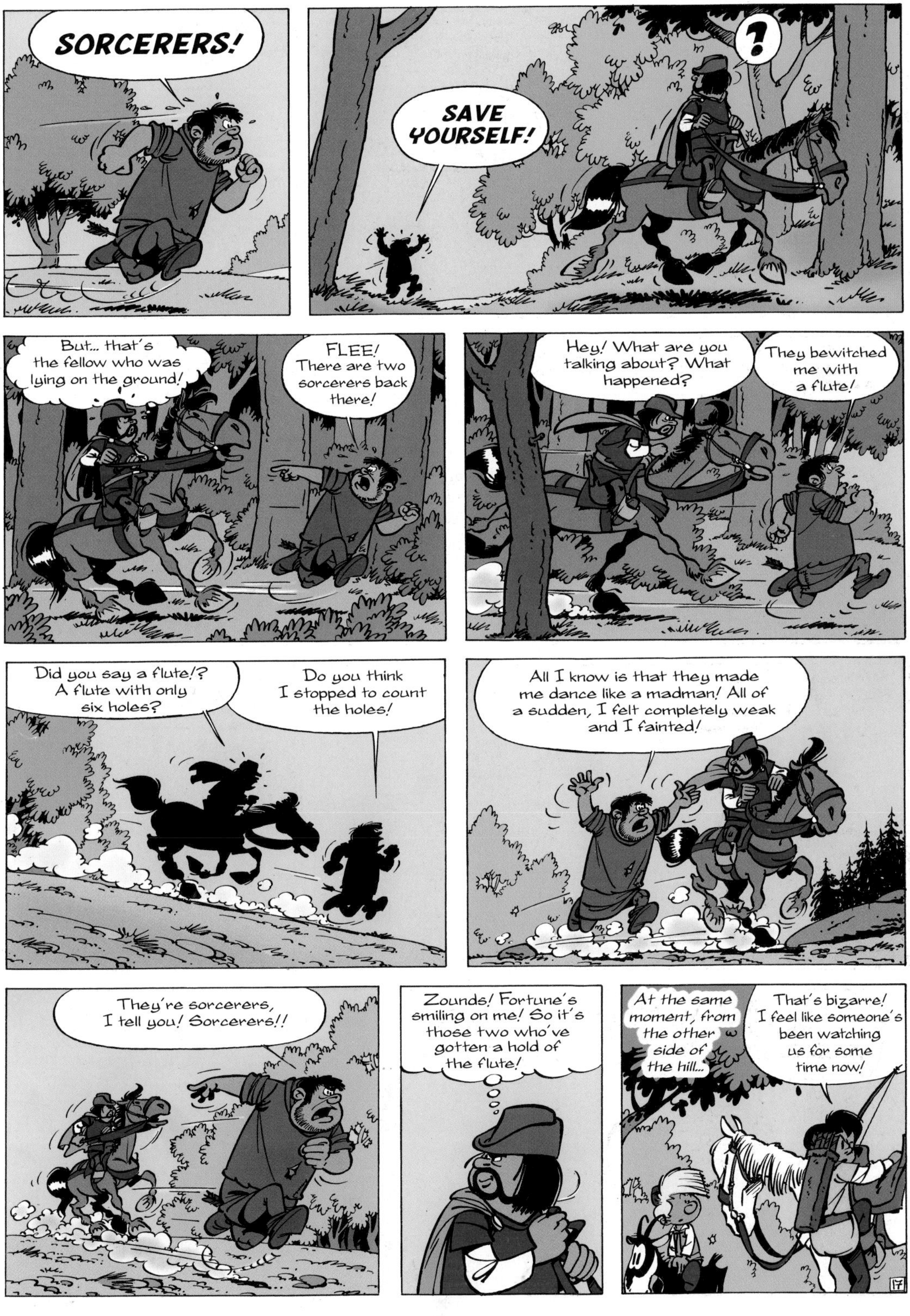

SORCERERS!
SAVE YOURSELF!
?
But... that's the fellow who was lying on the ground!
FLEE! There are two sorcerers back there!
Hey! What are you talking about? What happened?
They bewitched me with a flute!
Did you say a flute!? A flute with only six holes?
Do you think I stopped to count the holes!
All I know is that they made me dance like a madman! All of a sudden, I felt completely weak and I fainted!
They're sorcerers, I tell you! Sorcerers!!
Zounds! Fortune's smiling on me! So it's those two who've gotten a hold of the flute!
At the same moment, from the other side of the hill...
That's bizarre! I feel like someone's been watching us for some time now!
17

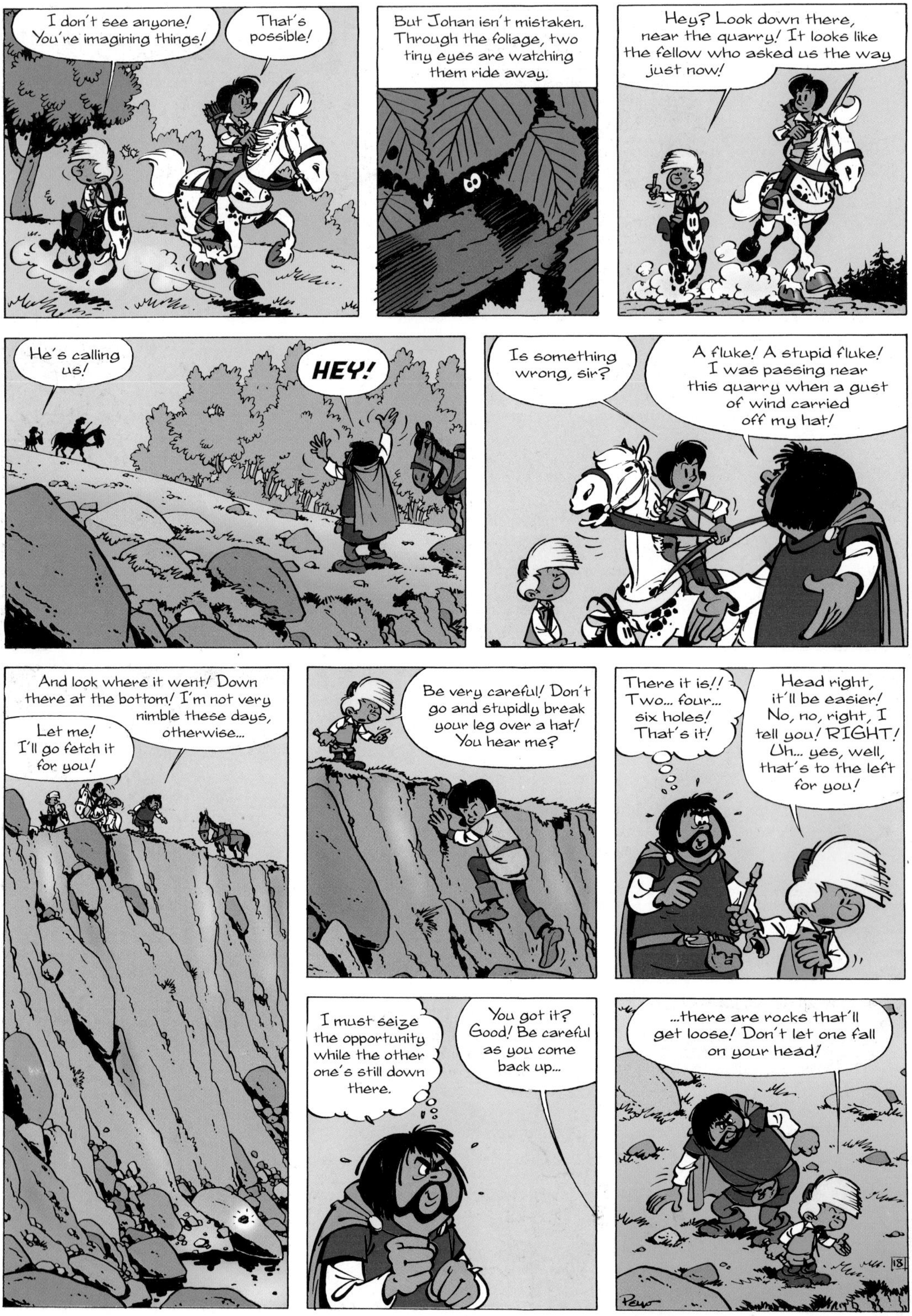
I don't see anyone! You're imagining things!
That's possible!
But Johan isn't mistaken. Through the foliage, two tiny eyes are watching them ride away.
Hey? Look down there, near the quarry! It looks like the fellow who asked us the way just now!
He's calling us!
HEY!
Is something wrong, sir?
A fluke! A stupid fluke! I was passing near this quarry when a gust of wind carried off my hat!
And look where it went! Down there at the bottom! I'm not very nimble these days, otherwise...
Let me! I'll go fetch it for you!
Be very careful! Don't go and stupidly break your leg over a hat! You hear me?
There it is!! Two... four... six holes! That's it!
Head right, it'll be easier! No, no, right, I tell you! RIGHT! Uh... yes, well, that's to the left for you!
I must seize the opportunity while the other one's still down there.
You got it? Good! Be careful as you come back up...
...there are rocks that'll get loose! Don't let one fall on your head!
18

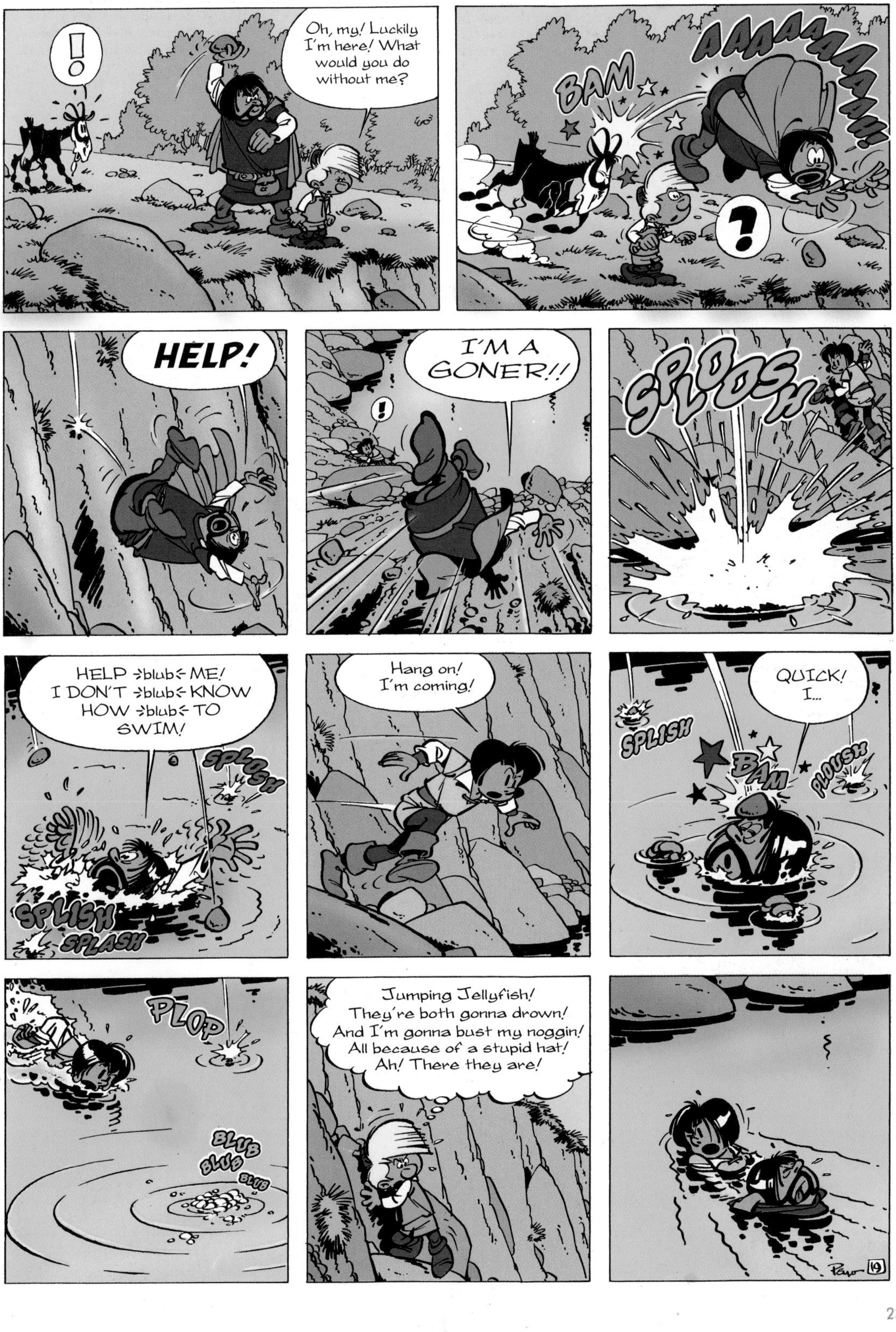

!
Oh, my! Luckily I'm here! What would you do without me?
BAM
AAAAAAAAAAH!
?
HELP!
I'M A GONER!!
!
SPLOOOSH
HELP >blub< ME! I DON'T >blub< KNOW HOW >blub< TO SWIM!
SPLOSH
SPLISH
SPLASH
Hang on! I'm coming!
SPLISH
QUICK! I...
BAM
PLOUSH
PLOP
BLUB
BLUB
BLUB
Jumping Jellyfish! They're both gonna drown! And I'm gonna bust my noggin! All because of a stupid hat! Ah! There they are!
19

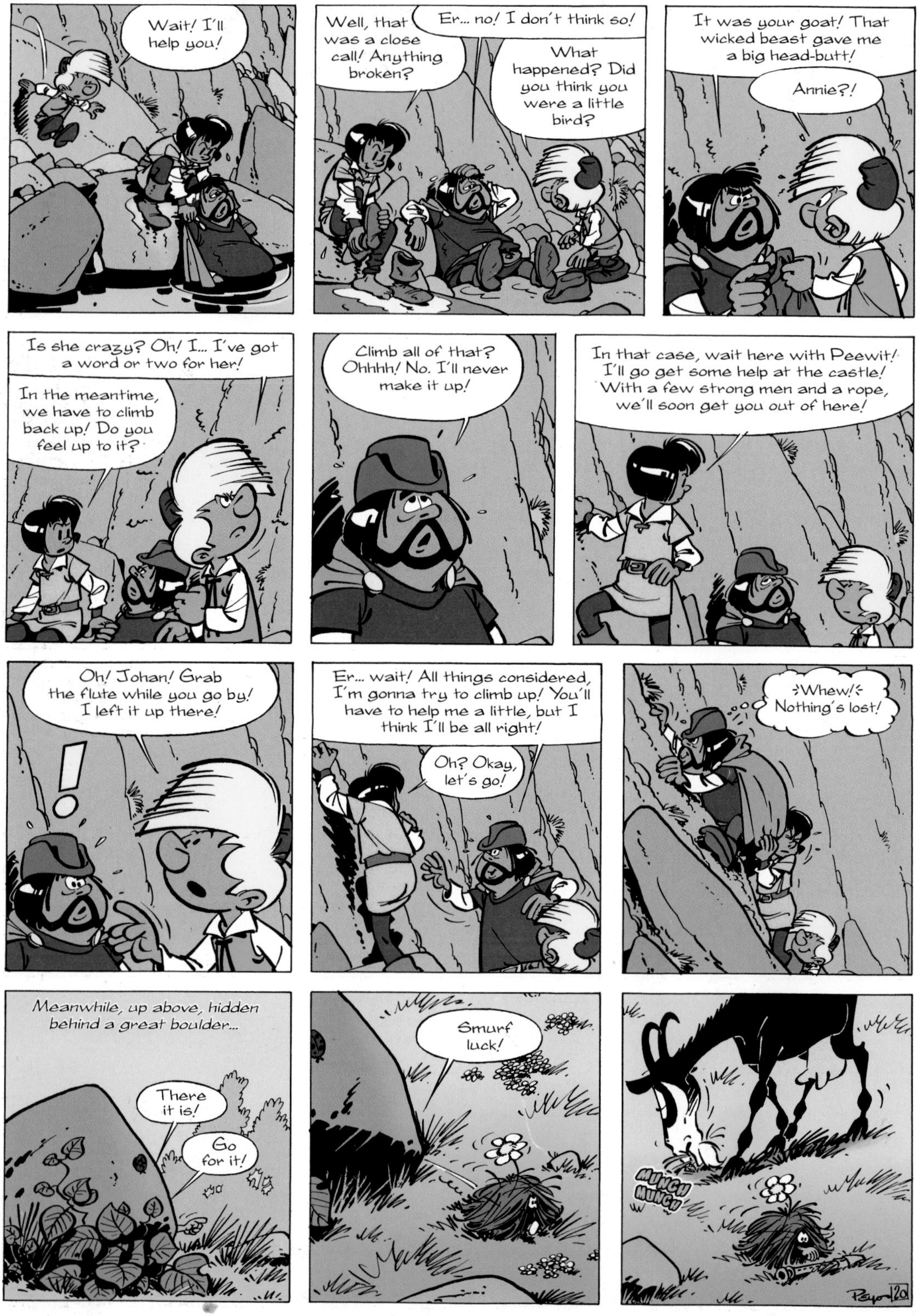

Wait! I'll help you!
Well, that was a close call! Anything broken?
Er... no! I don't think so!
What happened? Did you think you were a little bird?
It was your goat! That wicked beast gave me a big head-butt!
Annie?!
Is she crazy? Oh! I... I've got a word or two for her!
In the meantime, we have to climb back up! Do you feel up to it?
Climb all of that? Ohhhh! No. I'll never make it up!
In that case, wait here with Peewit! I'll go get some help at the castle! With a few strong men and a rope, we'll soon get you out of here!
Oh! Johan! Grab the flute while you go by! I left it up there!
!
Er... wait! All things considered, I'm gonna try to climb up! You'll have to help me a little, but I think I'll be all right!
Oh? Okay, let's go!
Whew! Nothing's lost!
Meanwhile, up above, hidden behind a great boulder...
There it is!
Go for it!
Smurf luck!
MUNCH
MUNCH
Peyo 20

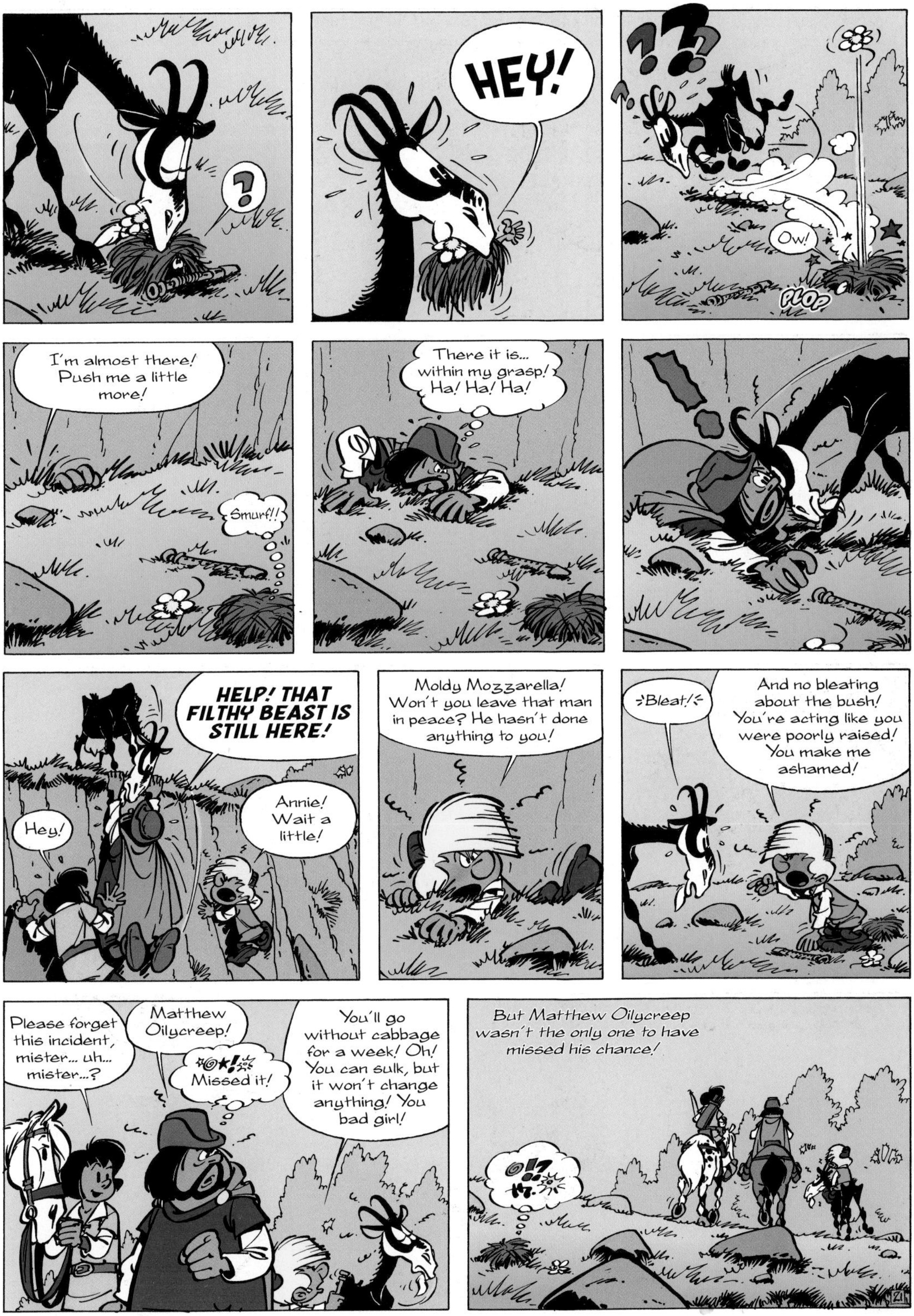

?
HEY!
Ow!
PLOP
I'm almost there! Push me a little more!
Smurf!!
There it is... within my grasp! Ha! Ha! Ha!
HELP! THAT FILTHY BEAST IS STILL HERE!
Hey!
Annie! Wait a little!
Moldy Mozzarella! Won't you leave that man in peace? He hasn't done anything to you!
Bleat!
And no bleating about the bush! You're acting like you were poorly raised! You make me ashamed!
Please forget this incident, mister... uh... mister...?
Matthew Oilycreep!
Missed it!
You'll go without cabbage for a week! Oh! You can sulk, but it won't change anything! You bad girl!
But Matthew Oilycreep wasn't the only one to have missed his chance!

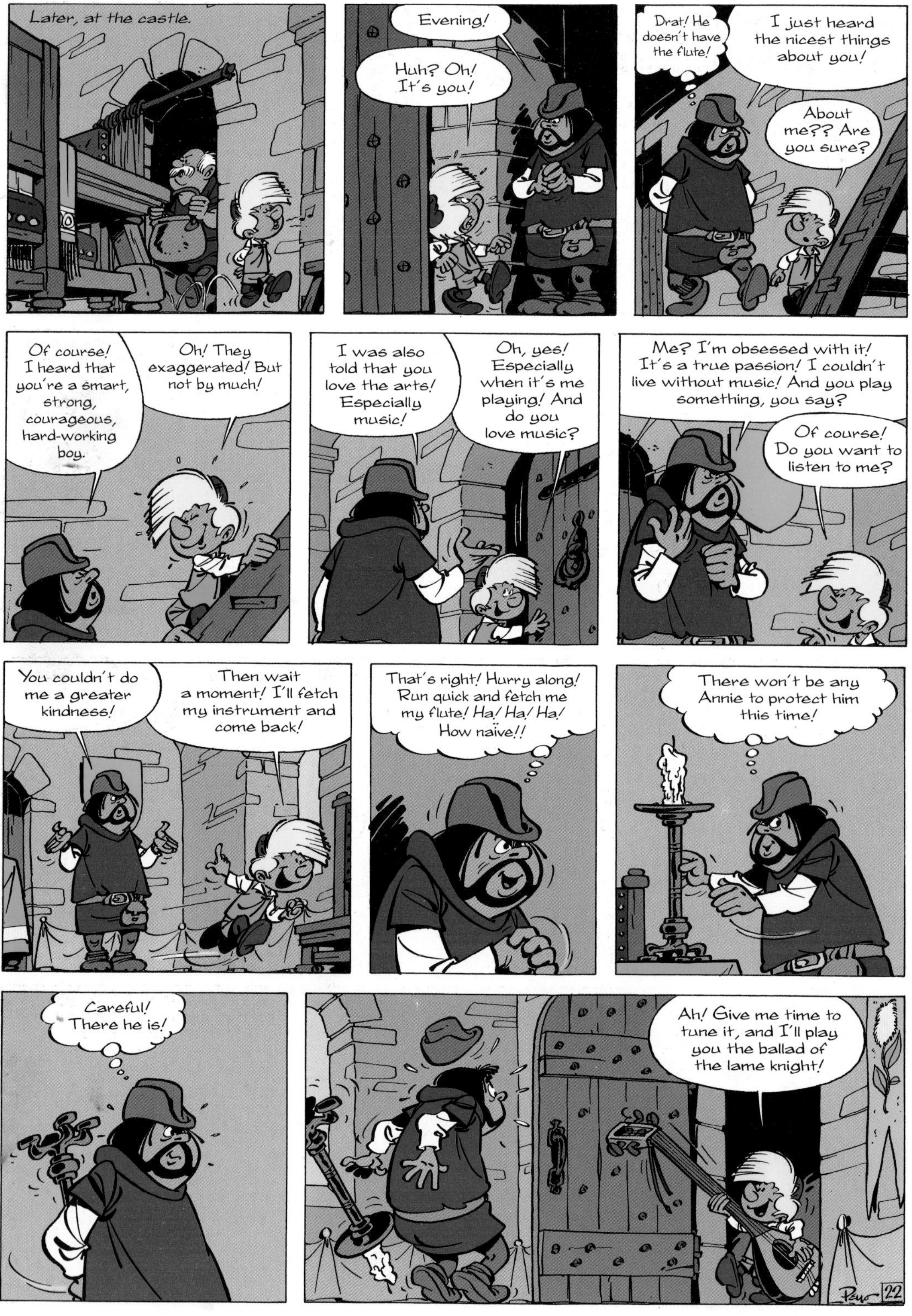
Later, at the castle.
Evening!
Huh? Oh! It's you!
Drat! He doesn't have the flute!
I just heard the nicest things about you!
About me?? Are you sure?
Of course! I heard that you're a smart, strong, courageous, hard-working boy.
Oh! They exaggerated! But not by much!
I was also told that you love the arts! Especially music!
Oh, yes! Especially when it's me playing! And do you love music?
Me? I'm obsessed with it! It's a true passion! I couldn't live without music! And you play something, you say?
Of course! Do you want to listen to me?
You couldn't do me a greater kindness!
Then wait a moment! I'll fetch my instrument and come back!
That's right! Hurry along! Run quick and fetch me my flute! Ha! Ha! Ha! How naïve!!
There won't be any Annie to protect him this time!
Careful! There he is!
Ah! Give me time to tune it, and I'll play you the ballad of the lame knight!
22

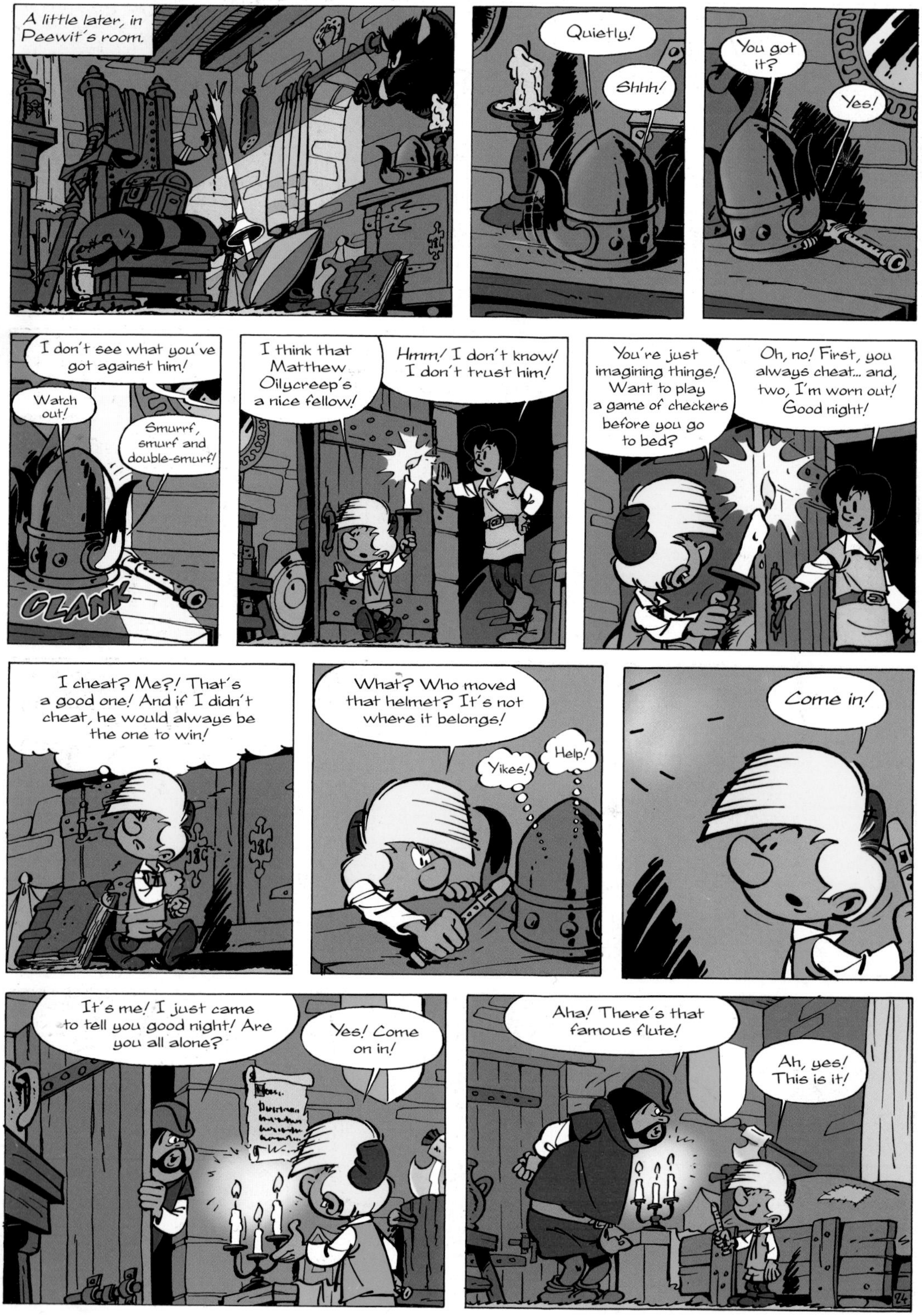
A little later, in Peewit's room.
Quietly!
Shhh!
You got it?
Yes!
I don't see what you've got against him!
Watch out!
Smurf, smurf and double-smurf!
CLANK
I think that Matthew Oilycreep's a nice fellow!
Hmm! I don't know! I don't trust him!
You're just imagining things! Want to play a game of checkers before you go to bed?
Oh, no! First, you always cheat... and, two, I'm worn out! Good night!
I cheat? Me?! That's a good one! And if I didn't cheat, he would always be the one to win!
What? Who moved that helmet? It's not where it belongs!
Yikes!
Help!
Come in!
It's me! I just came to tell you good night! Are you all alone?
Yes! Come on in!
Aha! There's that famous flute!
Ah, yes! This is it!

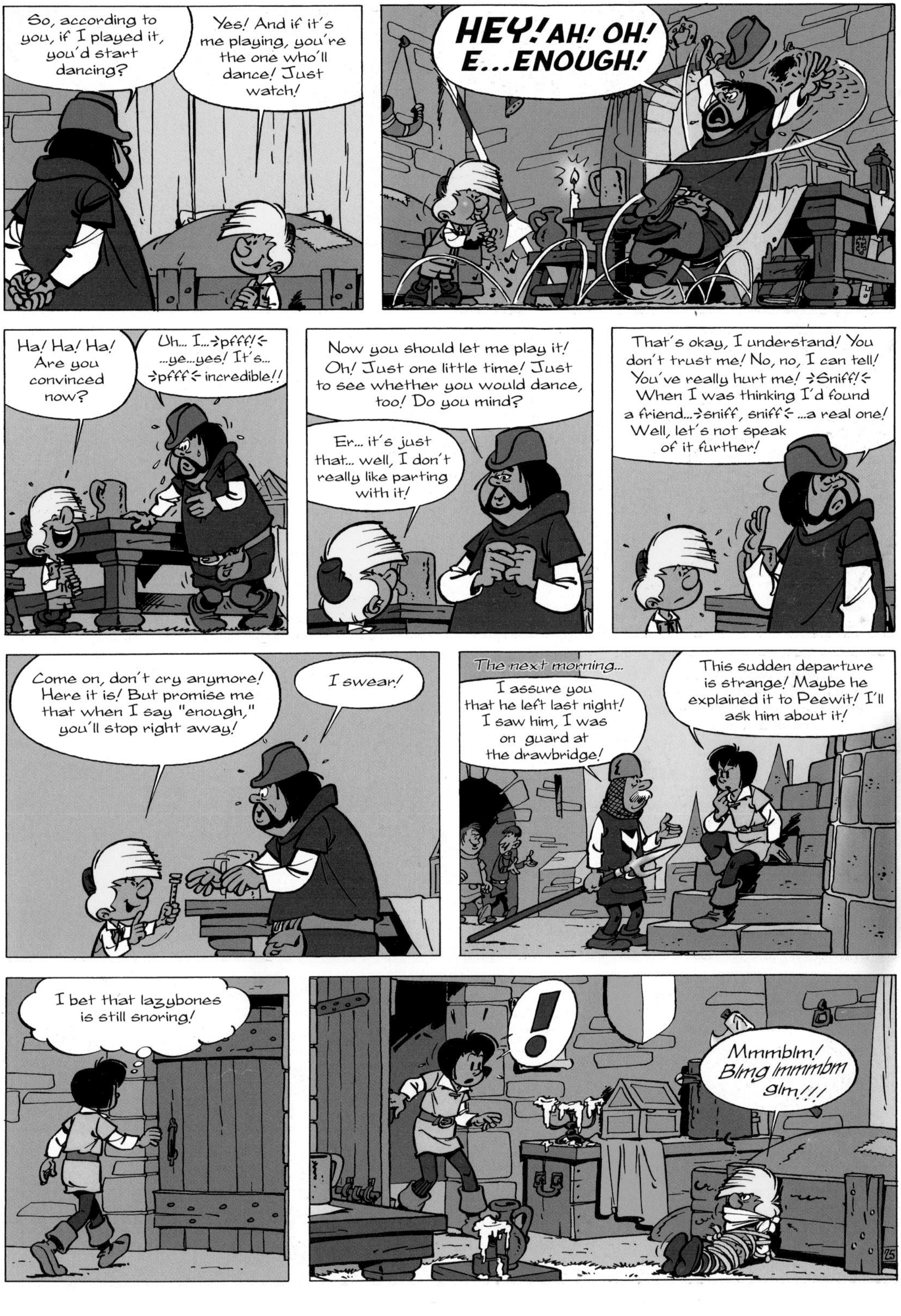
So, according to you, if I played it, you'd start dancing?
Yes! And if it's me playing, you're the one who'll dance! Just watch!
HEY! AH! OH! E...ENOUGH!
Ha! Ha! Ha! Are you convinced now?
Uh... I...→pfff!← ...ye...yes! It's... →pfff← incredible!!
Now you should let me play it! Oh! Just one little time! Just to see whether you would dance, too! Do you mind?
Er... it's just that... well, I don't really like parting with it!
That's okay, I understand! You don't trust me! No, no, I can tell! You've really hurt me! →Sniff!← When I was thinking I'd found a friend...→sniff, sniff← ...a real one! Well, let's not speak of it further!
Come on, don't cry anymore! Here it is! But promise me that when I say "enough," you'll stop right away!
I swear!
The next morning...
I assure you that he left last night! I saw him, I was on guard at the drawbridge!
This sudden departure is strange! Maybe he explained it to Peewit! I'll ask him about it!
I bet that lazybones is still snoring!
!
Mmmblm! Blmg lmmmbm glm!!!

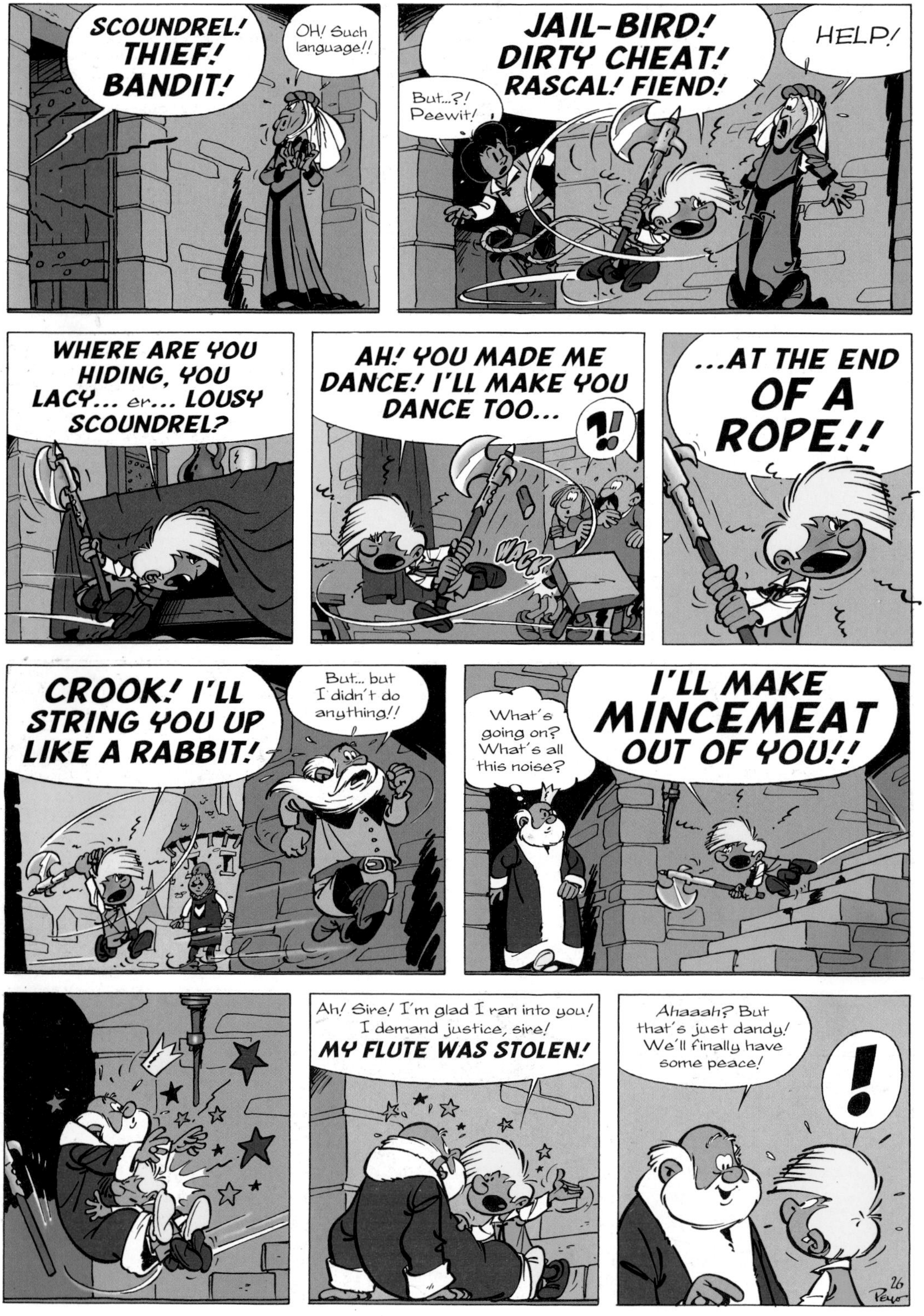

SCOUNDREL! THIEF! BANDIT!
OH! Such language!!
JAIL-BIRD! DIRTY CHEAT! RASCAL! FIEND!
But...?! Peewit!
HELP!
WHERE ARE YOU HIDING, YOU LACY... er... LOUSY SCOUNDREL?
AH! YOU MADE ME DANCE! I'LL MAKE YOU DANCE TOO...
!!
WACK
...AT THE END OF A ROPE!!
CROOK! I'LL STRING YOU UP LIKE A RABBIT!
But... but I didn't do anything!!
What's going on? What's all this noise?
I'LL MAKE MINCEMEAT OUT OF YOU!!
Ah! Sire! I'm glad I ran into you! I demand justice, sire! MY FLUTE WAS STOLEN!
Ahaaah? But that's just dandy! We'll finally have some peace!
!
26
Peyo

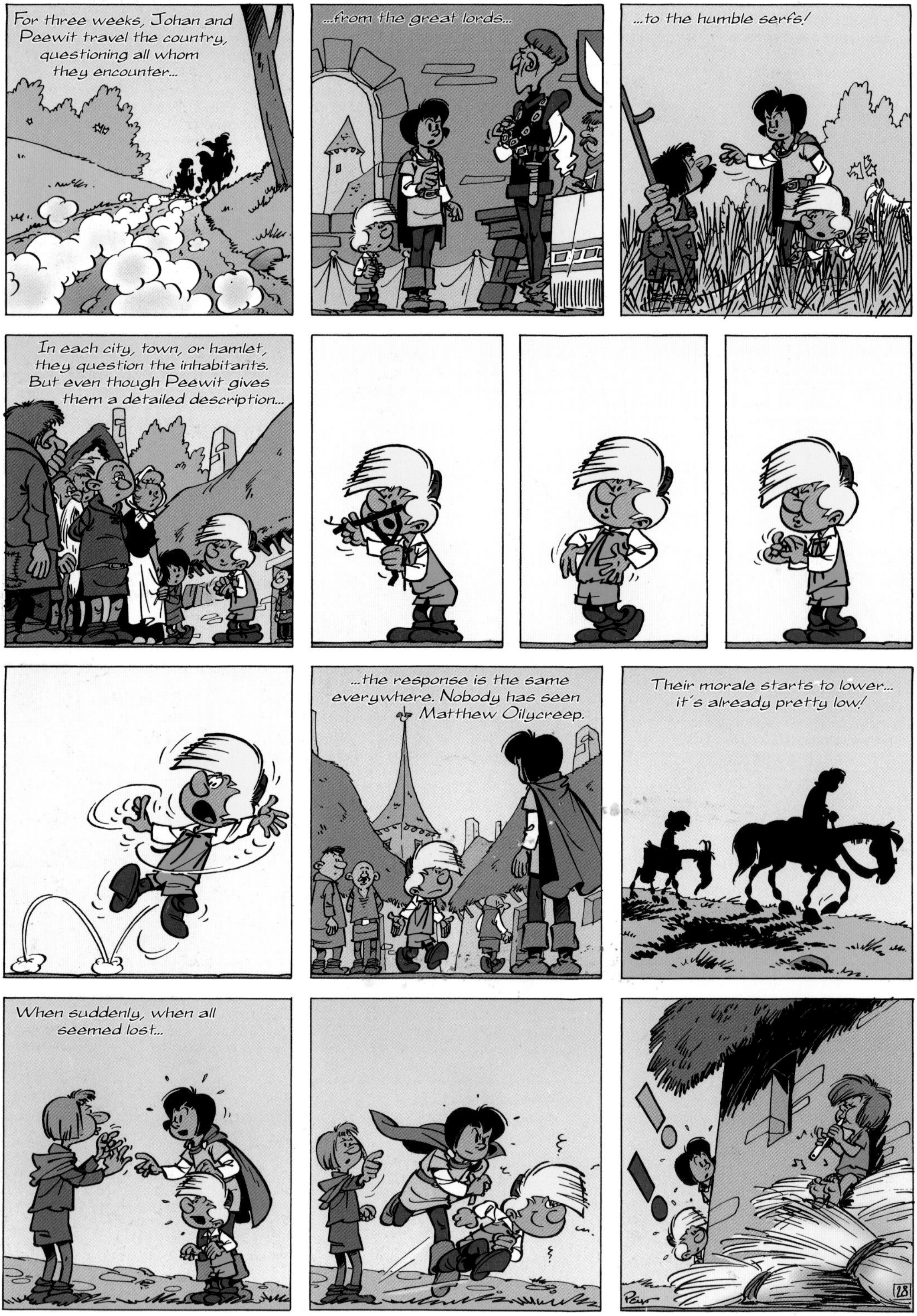
For three weeks, Johan and Peewit travel the country, questioning all whom they encounter...
...from the great lords...
...to the humble serfs!
In each city, town, or hamlet, they question the inhabitants. But even though Peewit gives them a detailed description...
...the response is the same everywhere. Nobody has seen Matthew Oilycreep.
Their morale starts to lower... it's already pretty low!
When suddenly, when all seemed lost...
28

34

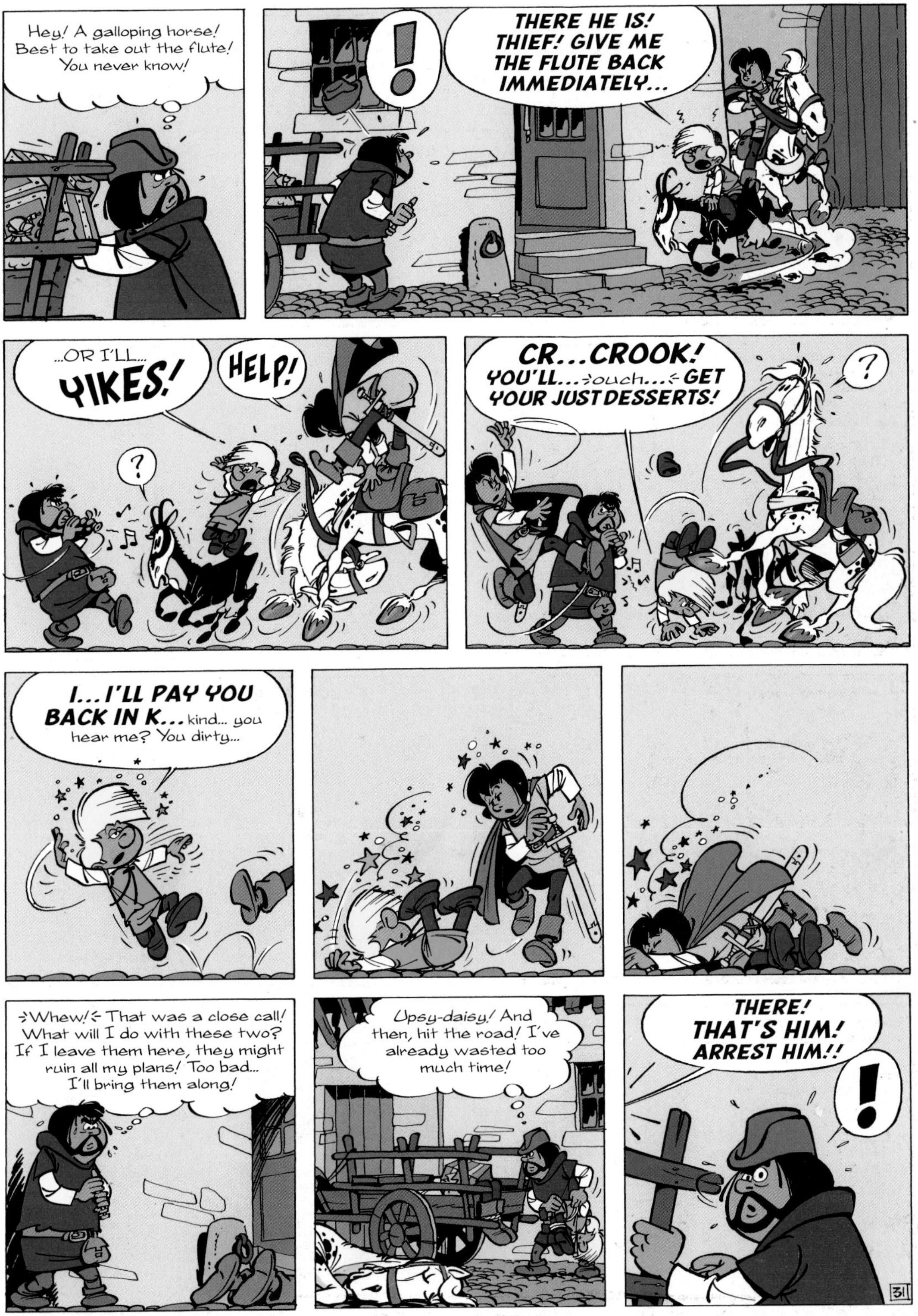

Hey! A galloping horse! Best to take out the flute! You never know!
!
THERE HE IS! THIEF! GIVE ME THE FLUTE BACK IMMEDIATELY...
...OR I'LL... YIKES!
HELP!
?
CR...CROOK! YOU'LL... ouch... GET YOUR JUST DESSERTS!
?
I...I'LL PAY YOU BACK IN K... kind... you hear me? You dirty...
Whew! That was a close call! What will I do with these two? If I leave them here, they might ruin all my plans! Too bad... I'll bring them along!
Upsy-daisy! And then, hit the road! I've already wasted too much time!
THERE! THAT'S HIM! ARREST HIM!!
!
31

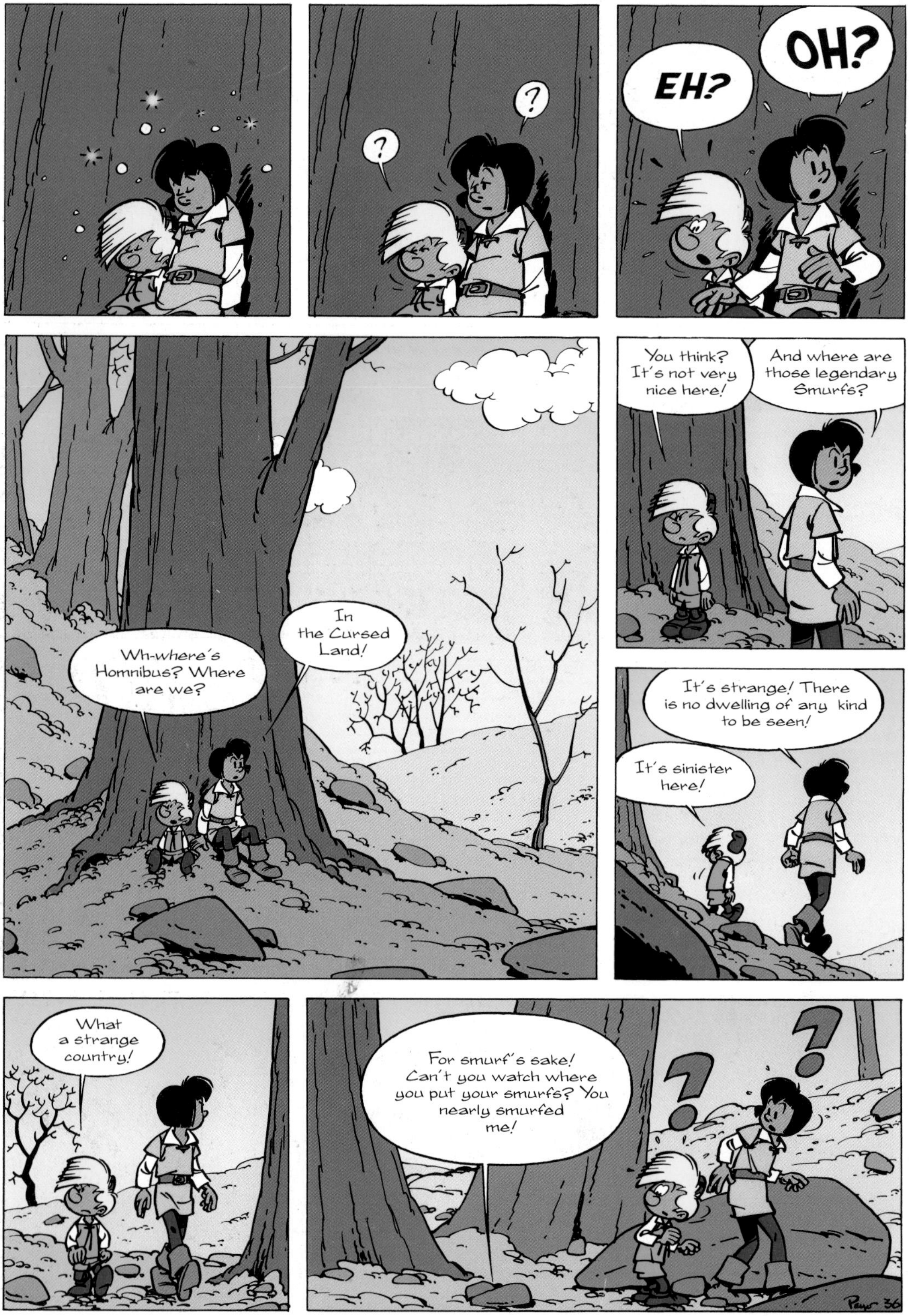
?
?
EH?
OH?
Wh-where's Homnibus? Where are we?
In the Cursed Land!
You think? It's not very nice here!
And where are those legendary Smurfs?
It's strange! There is no dwelling of any kind to be seen!
It's sinister here!
What a strange country!
For smurf's sake! Can't you watch where you put your smurfs? You nearly smurfed me!
?
?
Peyo 36

41

45

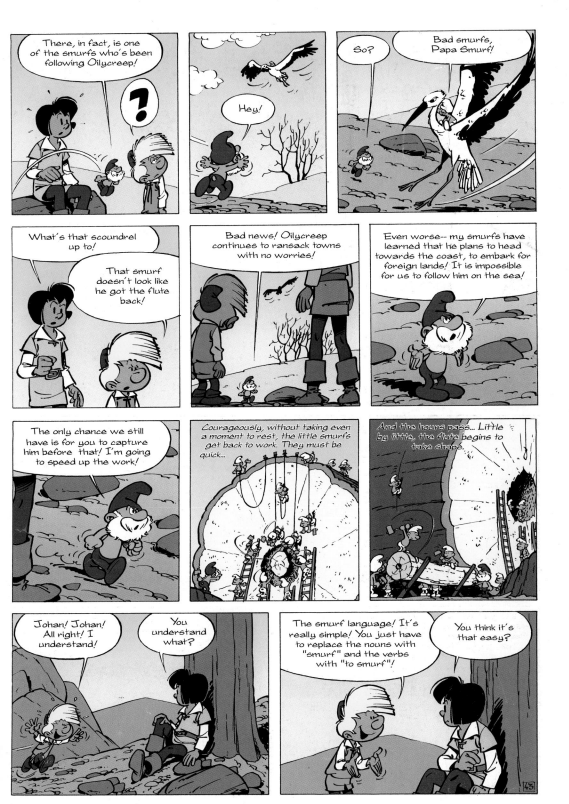

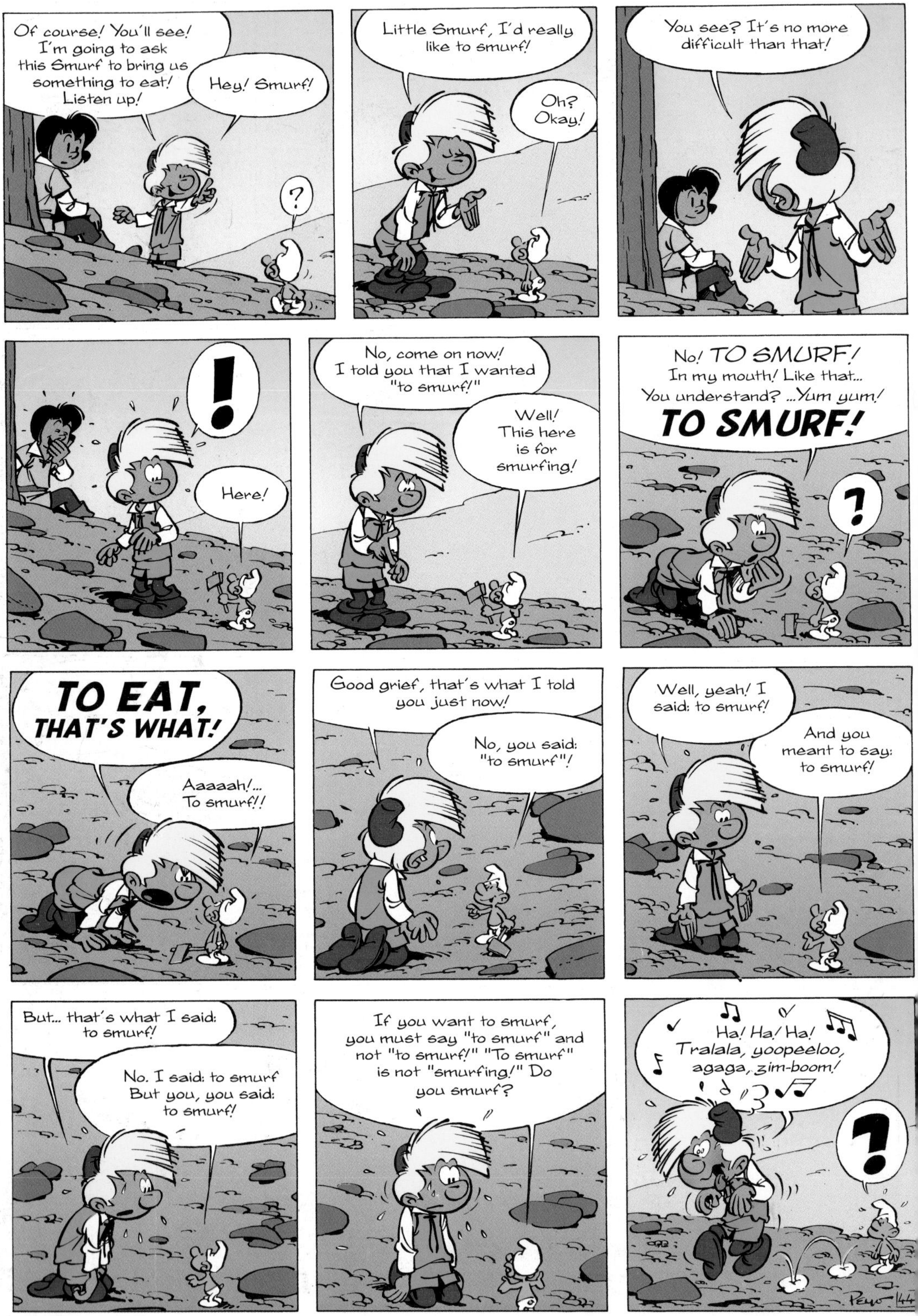
Of course! You'll see! I'm going to ask this Smurf to bring us something to eat! Listen up!
Hey! Smurf!
?
Little Smurf, I'd really like to smurf!
Oh? Okay!
You see? It's no more difficult than that!
!
Here!
No, come on now! I told you that I wanted "to smurf!"
Well! This here is for smurfing!
No! TO SMURF! In my mouth! Like that... You understand? ...Yum yum! TO SMURF!
?
TO EAT, THAT'S WHAT!
Aaaaah!... To smurf!!
Good grief, that's what I told you just now!
No, you said: "to smurf"!
Well, yeah! I said: to smurf!
And you meant to say: to smurf!
But... that's what I said: to smurf!
No. I said: to smurf But you, you said: to smurf!
If you want to smurf, you must say "to smurf" and not "to smurf!" "To smurf" is not "smurfing!" Do you smurf?
Ha! Ha! Ha! Tralala, yoopeeloo, agaga, zim-boom!
?

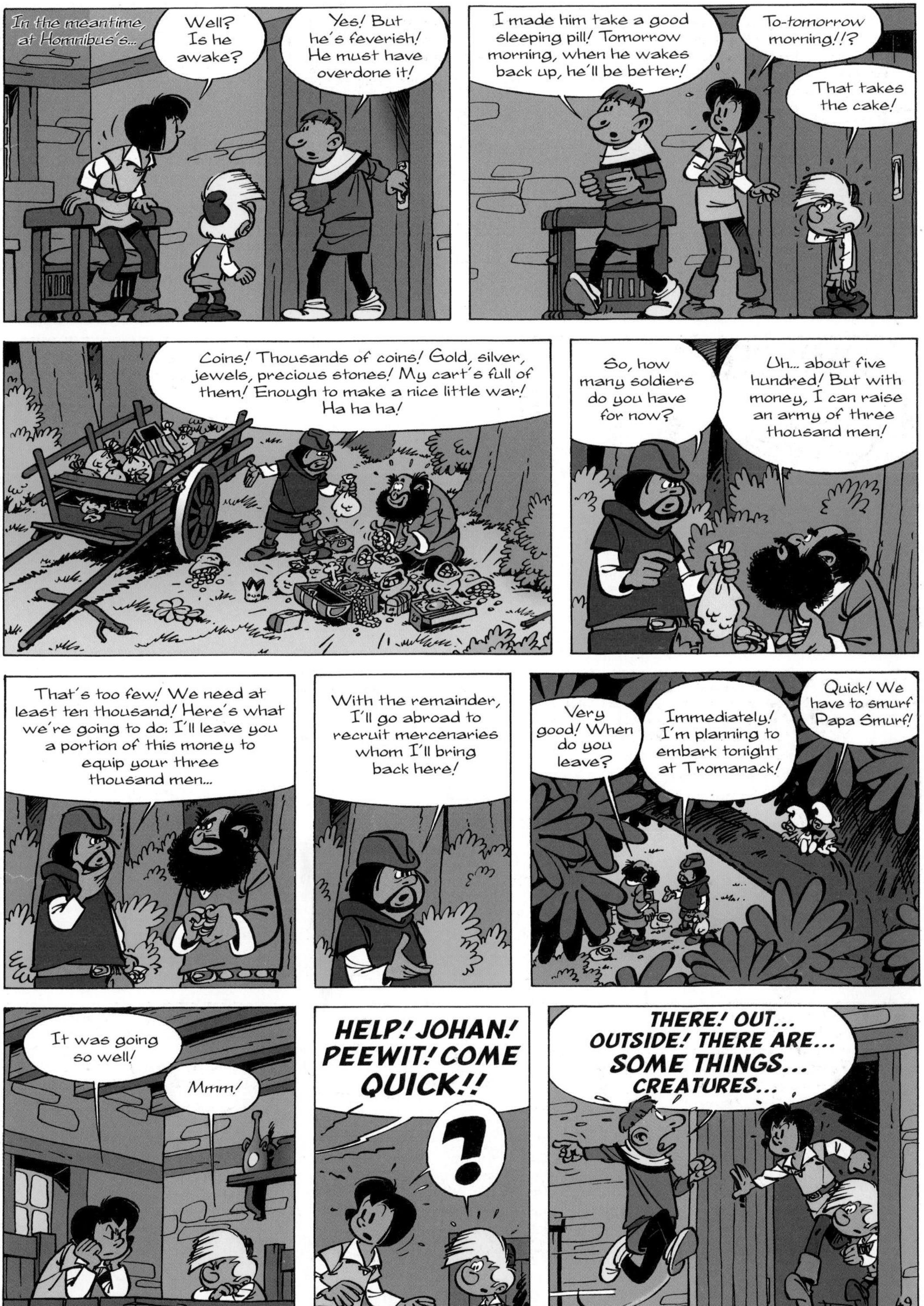

In the meantime, at Homnibus's...
Well? Is he awake?
Yes! But he's feverish! He must have overdone it!
I made him take a good sleeping pill! Tomorrow morning, when he wakes back up, he'll be better!
To-tomorrow morning!!?
That takes the cake!
Coins! Thousands of coins! Gold, silver, jewels, precious stones! My cart's full of them! Enough to make a nice little war! Ha ha ha!
So, how many soldiers do you have for now?
Uh... about five hundred! But with money, I can raise an army of three thousand men!
That's too few! We need at least ten thousand! Here's what we're going to do: I'll leave you a portion of this money to equip your three thousand men...
With the remainder, I'll go abroad to recruit mercenaries whom I'll bring back here!
Very good! When do you leave?
Immediately! I'm planning to embark tonight at Tromanack!
Quick! We have to smurf Papa Smurf!
It was going so well!
Mmm!
HELP! JOHAN! PEEWIT! COME QUICK!!
?
THERE! OUT... OUTSIDE! THERE ARE... SOME THINGS... CREATURES...
49

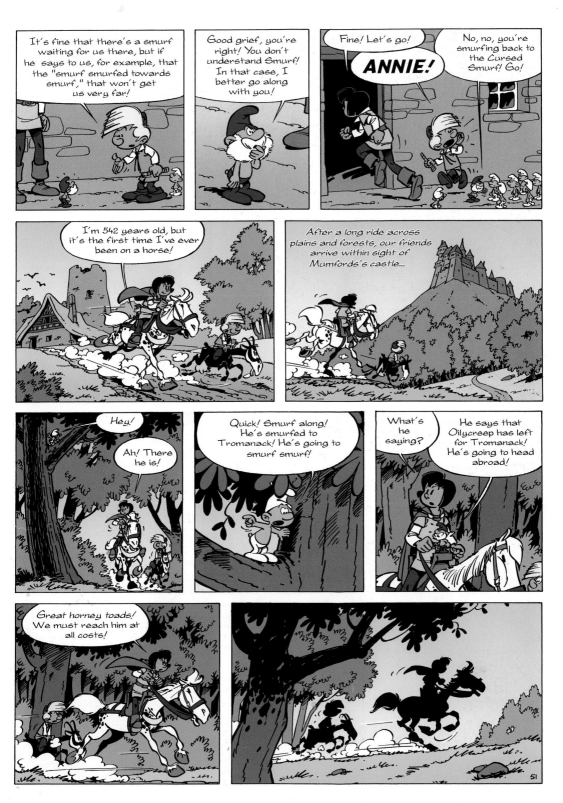

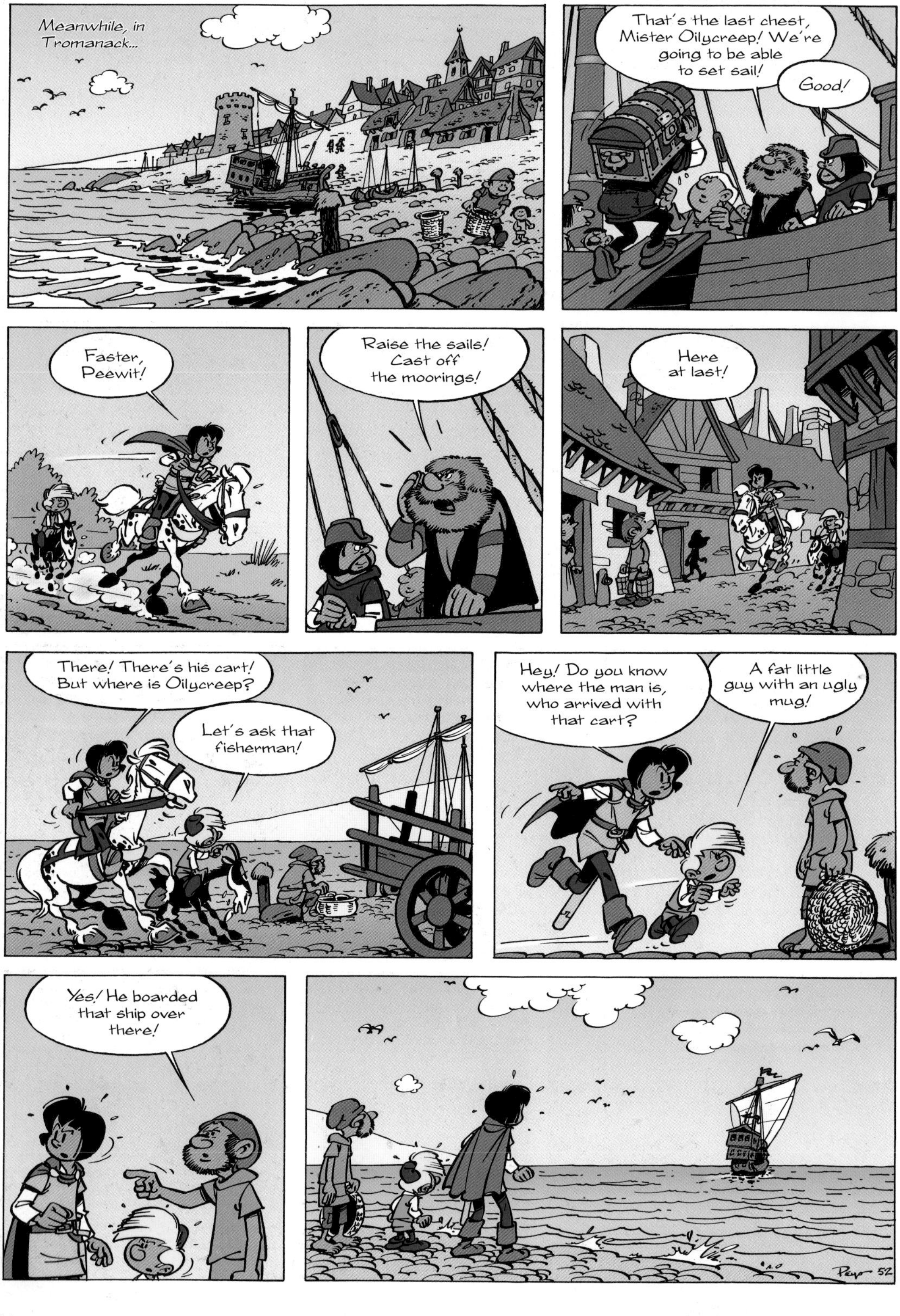

Meanwhile, in Tromanack...
That's the last chest, Mister Oilycreep! We're going to be able to set sail!
Good!
Faster, Peewit!
Raise the sails! Cast off the moorings!
Here at last!
There! There's his cart! But where is Oilycreep?
Let's ask that fisherman!
Hey! Do you know where the man is, who arrived with that cart?
A fat little guy with an ugly mug!
Yes! He boarded that ship over there!
Peyo 52

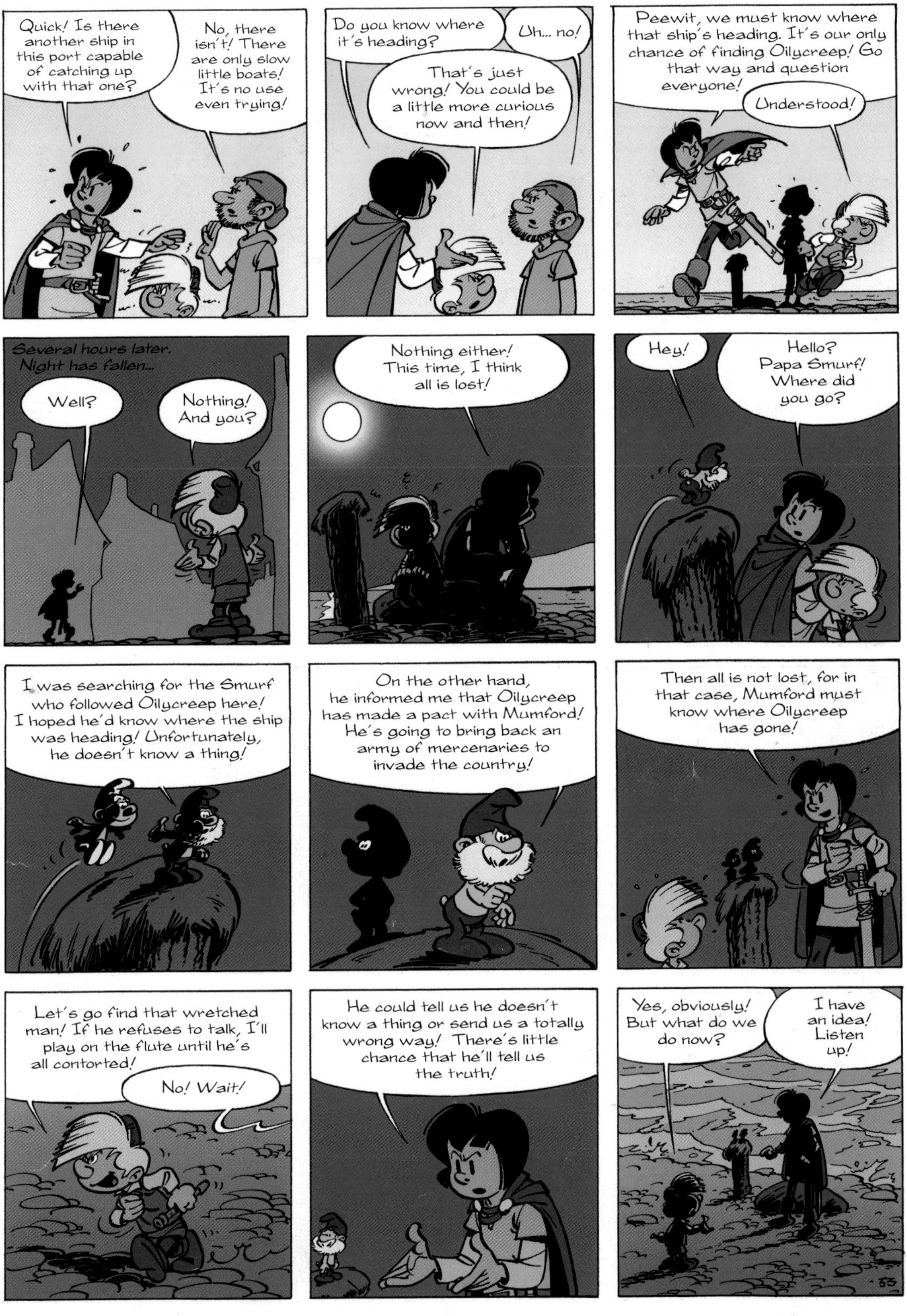
Quick! Is there another ship in this port capable of catching up with that one?
No, there isn't! There are only slow little boats! It's no use even trying!
Do you know where it's heading?
Uh... no!
That's just wrong! You could be a little more curious now and then!
Peewit, we must know where that ship's heading. It's our only chance of finding Oilycreep! Go that way and question everyone!
Understood!
Several hours later. Night has fallen...
Well?
Nothing! And you?
Nothing either! This time, I think all is lost!
Hey!
Hello? Papa Smurf! Where did you go?
I was searching for the Smurf who followed Oilycreep here! I hoped he'd know where the ship was heading! Unfortunately, he doesn't know a thing!
On the other hand, he informed me that Oilycreep has made a pact with Mumford! He's going to bring back an army of mercenaries to invade the country!
Then all is not lost, for in that case, Mumford must know where Oilycreep has gone!
Let's go find that wretched man! If he refuses to talk, I'll play on the flute until he's all contorted!
No! Wait!
He could tell us he doesn't know a thing or send us a totally wrong way! There's little chance that he'll tell us the truth!
Yes, obviously! But what do we do now?
I have an idea! Listen up!
53

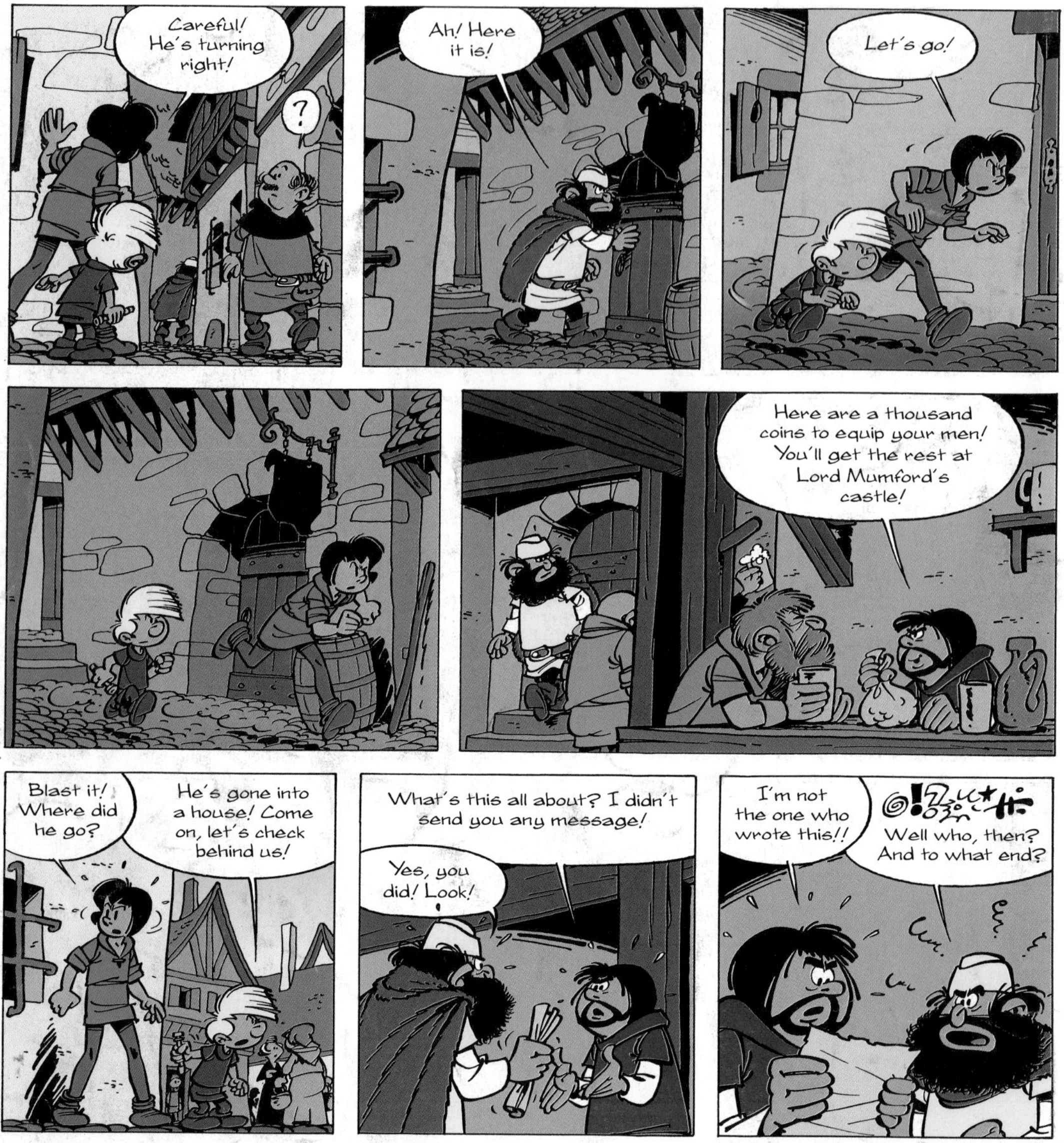
Careful! He's turning right!
?
Ah! Here it is!
Let's go!
Here are a thousand coins to equip your men! You'll get the rest at Lord Mumford's castle!
Blast it! Where did he go?
He's gone into a house! Come on, let's check behind us!
What's this all about? I didn't send you any message!
Yes, you did! Look!
I'm not the one who wrote this!!
Well who, then? And to what end?
We'll find out from the fisherman who brought you here! He must be in cahoots with whoever wrote this message! Come!
He can't be far!

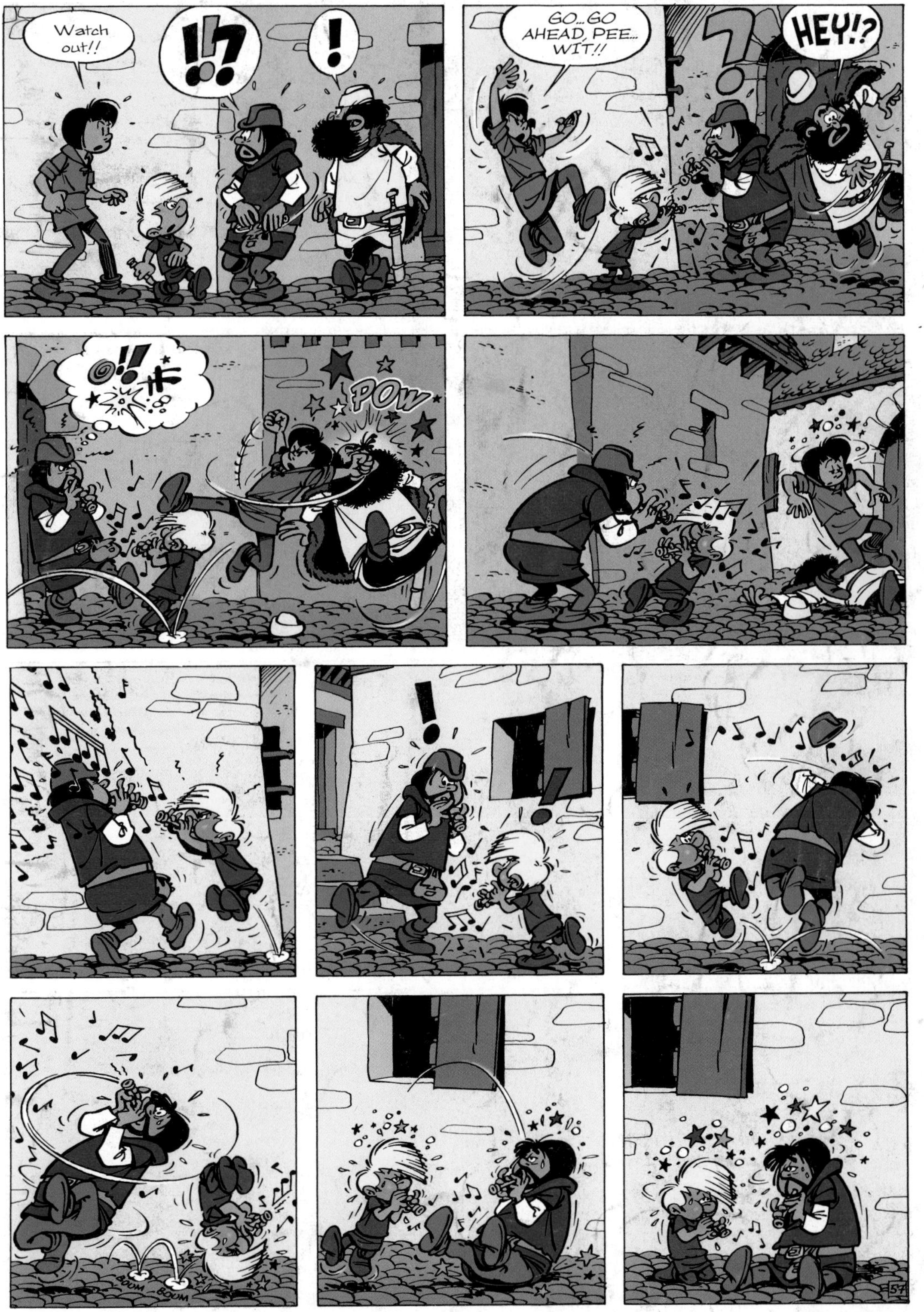
Watch out!!
!!?
!
GO...GO AHEAD, PEE... WIT!!
?
HEY!?
POW
BOOM BOOM
57

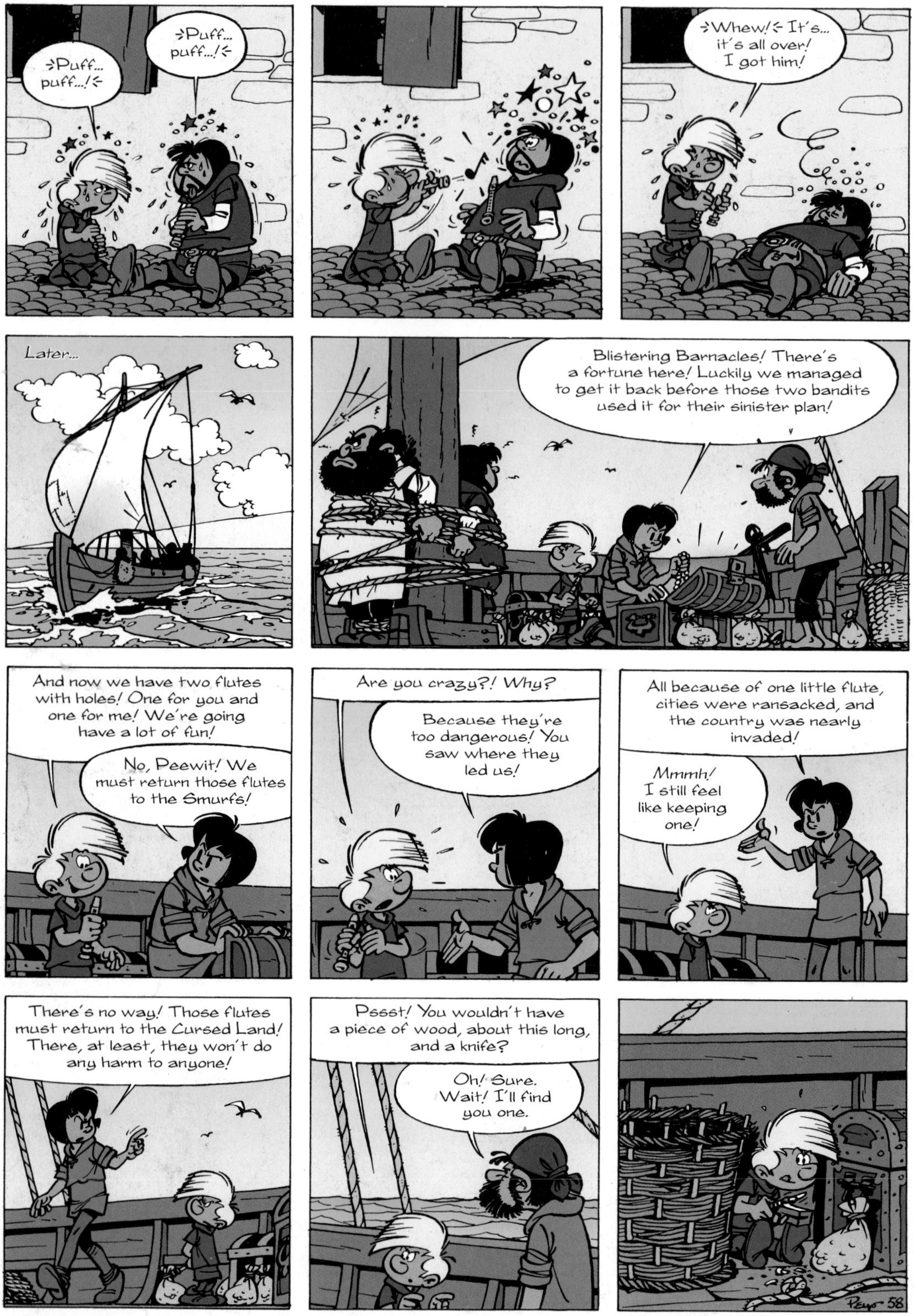

>Puff... puff...!<
>Puff... puff...!<
>Whew!< It's... it's all over! I got him!
Later...
Blistering Barnacles! There's a fortune here! Luckily we managed to get it back before those two bandits used it for their sinister plan!
And now we have two flutes with holes! One for you and one for me! We're going have a lot of fun!
No, Peewit! We must return those flutes to the Smurfs!
Are you crazy?! Why?
Because they're too dangerous! You saw where they led us!
All because of one little flute, cities were ransacked, and the country was nearly invaded!
Mmmh! I still feel like keeping one!
There's no way! Those flutes must return to the Cursed Land! There, at least, they won't do any harm to anyone!
Pssst! You wouldn't have a piece of wood, about this long, and a knife?
Oh! Sure. Wait! I'll find you one.
Peyo 58

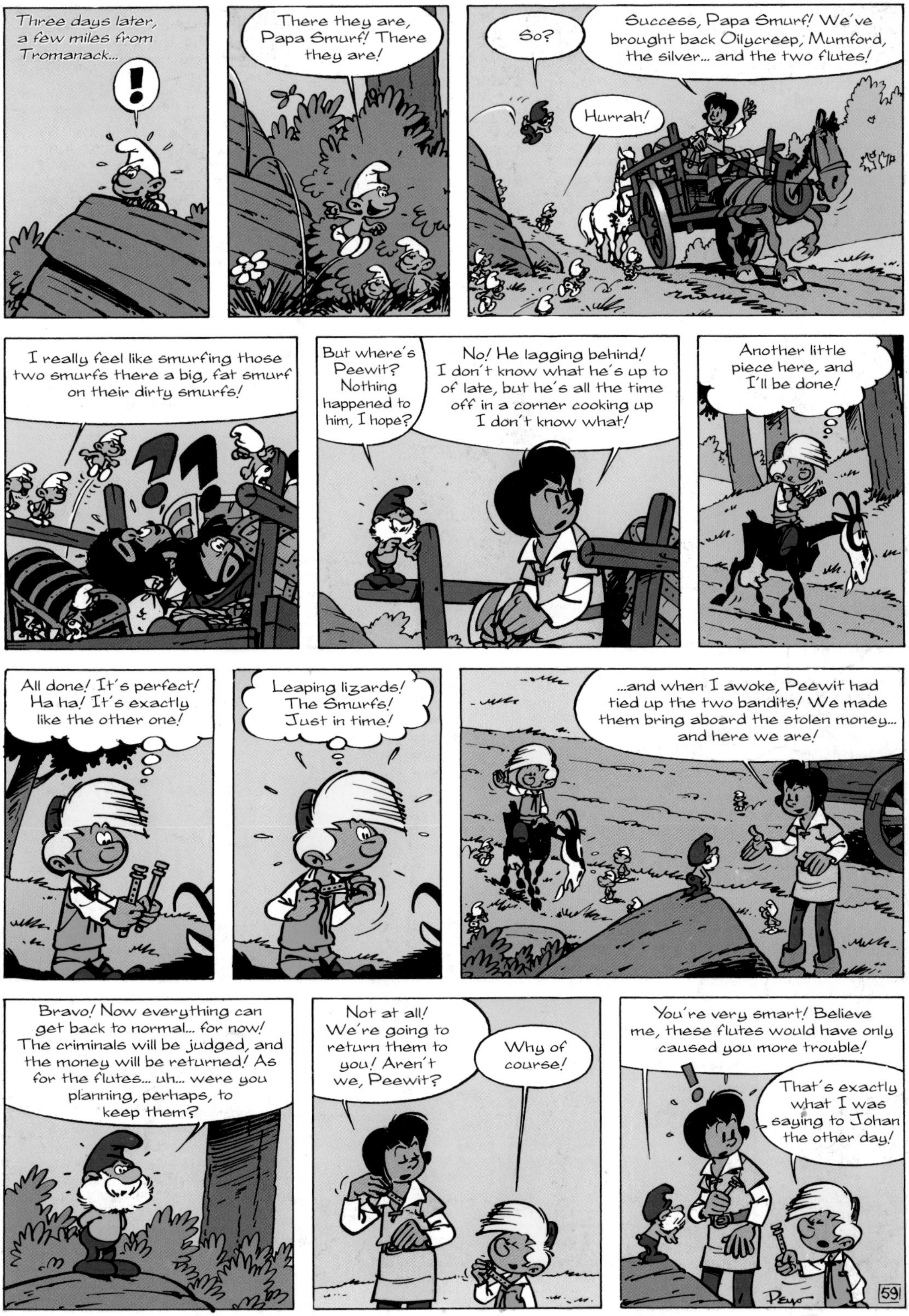

Three days later, a few miles from Tromanack...
!
There they are, Papa Smurf! There they are!
So?
Success, Papa Smurf! We've brought back Oilycreep, Mumford, the silver... and the two flutes!
Hurrah!
I really feel like smurfing those two smurfs there a big, fat smurf on their dirty smurfs!
But where's Peewit? Nothing happened to him, I hope?
No! He lagging behind! I don't know what he's up to of late, but he's all the time off in a corner cooking up I don't know what!
Another little piece here, and I'll be done!
All done! It's perfect! Ha ha! It's exactly like the other one!
Leaping lizards! The Smurfs! Just in time!
...and when I awoke, Peewit had tied up the two bandits! We made them bring aboard the stolen money... and here we are!
Bravo! Now everything can get back to normal... for now! The criminals will be judged, and the money will be returned! As for the flutes... uh... were you planning, perhaps, to keep them?
Not at all! We're going to return them to you! Aren't we, Peewit?
Why of course!
You're very smart! Believe me, these flutes would have only caused you more trouble!
!
That's exactly what I was saying to Johan the other day!
59
Peyo

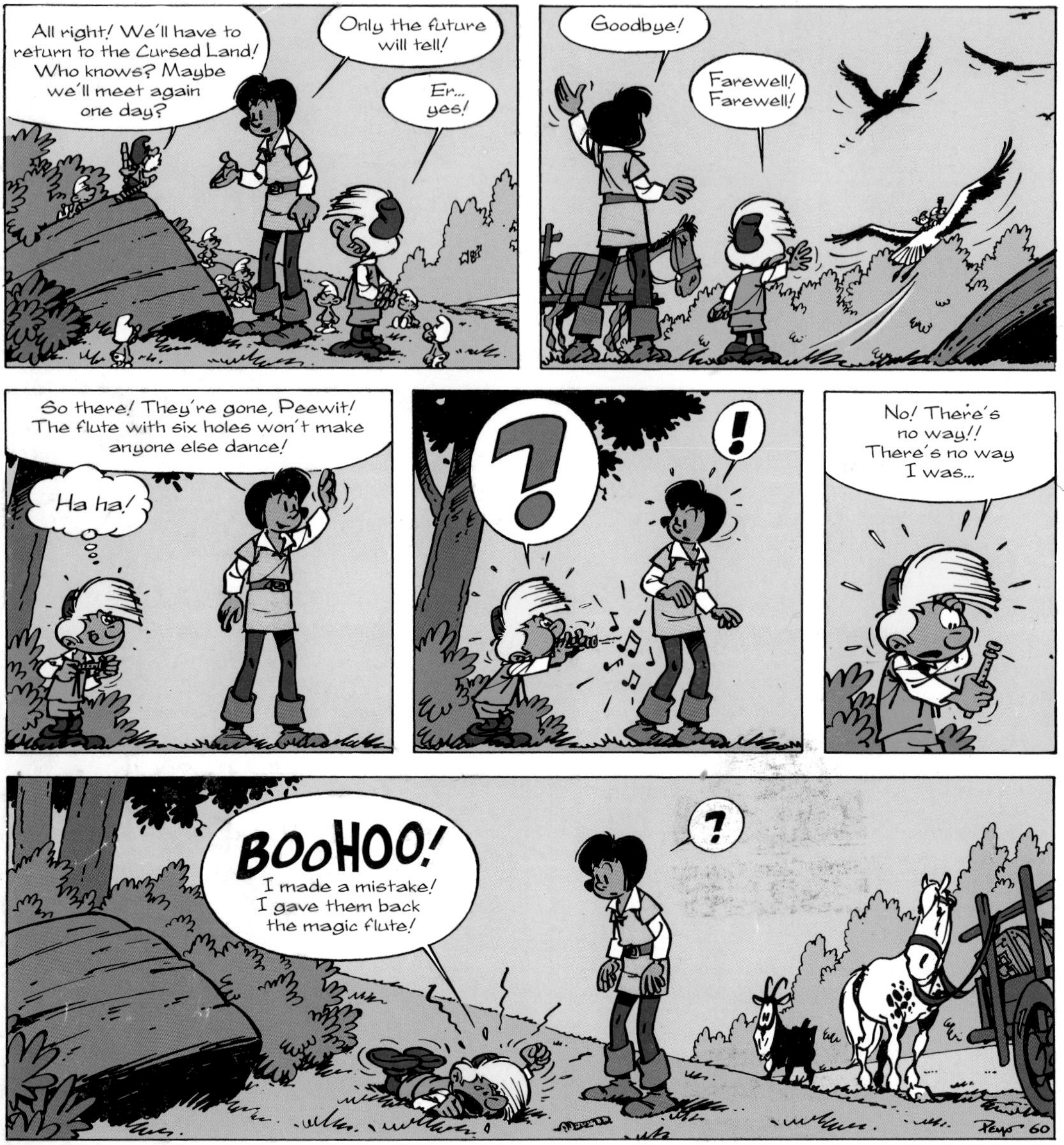
All right! We'll have to return to the Cursed Land! Who knows? Maybe we'll meet again one day?
Only the future will tell!
Er... yes!
Goodbye!
Farewell! Farewell!
So there! They're gone, Peewit! The flute with six holes won't make anyone else dance!
Ha ha!
?
!
No! There's no way!! There's no way I was...
BOOHOO! I made a mistake! I gave them back the magic flute!
?
Peyo 60

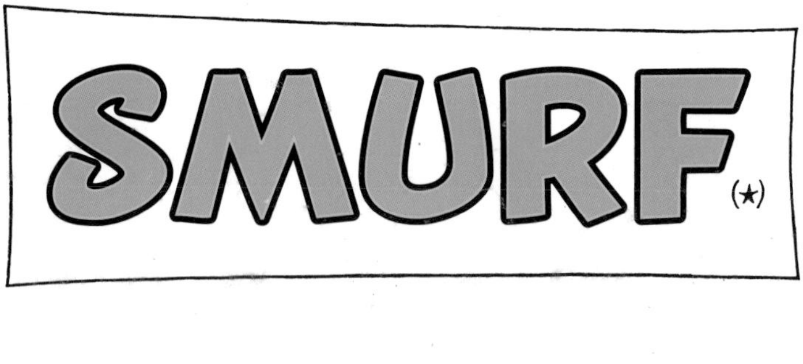
SMURF (★)

(★) THE END.